THE
LAST COLOR

Warm Regards
Vikas Khanna

THE
LAST COLOR

Vikas Khanna

BLOOMSBURY
NEW DELHI · LONDON · OXFORD · NEW YORK · SYDNEY

BLOOMSBURY INDIA
Bloomsbury Publishing India Pvt. Ltd
Second Floor, LSC Building No. 4, DDA Complex, Pocket C – 6 & 7,
Vasant Kunj, New Delhi 110070

BLOOMSBURY, BLOOMSBURY INDIA and the Diana logo are
trademarks of Bloomsbury Publishing Plc

First published 2018

Copyright © Vikas Khanna, 2018

All rights reserved. No part of this publication may be reproduced
or transmitted in any form or by any means, electronic or mechanical,
including photocopying, recording, or any information storage or
retrieval system, without prior permission in writing
from the publishers

Bloomsbury Publishing Plc does not have any control over, or
responsibility for, any third-party websites referred to or in this book.
All internet addresses given in this book were correct at the time of
going to press. The author and publisher regret any inconvenience
caused if addresses have changed or sites have ceased to exist,
but can accept no responsibility for any such changes

ISBN: 978-93-87863-21-7

2 4 6 8 10 9 7 5 3 1

Photo credits: Rajesh Kumar Singh

Printed and bound in India by Thomson Press India Ltd.

To find out more about our authors and books
visit www.bloomsbury.com and sign up for our newsletters

To,
The promise-keepers of friendship

Contents

Prologue – A Divided Birth ix

The River Back Home 1

Tamasha 25

Temple of Fireflies 49

The Birth of Light 69

The Legacy of Nothing 103

The Lost Spring 137

The Faces in the Shadows 167

A Pouch of Color 193

The Flower of Faded Orange 213

The Bird Flies 225

Epilogue 235

Acknowledgements 245

Prologue—A Divided Birth

A newborn was dumped face-down in the rotting heaps of garbage, left to fight for her survival amongst the rats and stray dogs and the refuse of society. Somehow no one, not one person, seemed to hear her cry. How could they? Their ears were hardened to the likes of her. What is the significance, after all, of a life struggling to be born in a city where people come to die?

It is said a baby's first cry is a celebration of the seamless, mostly colorless, sometimes odorless air that enters softly through her mouth and nose, to power her lungs and transform into life-giving breath. In Varanasi, this air is a potent combination of dust, sandalwood and rose-scented incense, the vibrations of chants and slokas, the mist of the Ganga, the death crackle of burning pyres and, of course, the spirit of survival.

But today, at this moment, this story, this life trembles on the edge of an echo.

It is believed that when Ravana was born he screamed so loud that his father Vishrava named him "Ravana" after the terrifying sound he made. But here, at this moment,

PROLOGUE—A DIVIDED BIRTH

even that terrifying roar would not have been heard amidst the honking and chanting.

For this vulnerable shame of society to survive, she would have to be louder. Louder than the chants and the temple's ringing bells, louder than the lung-challenging sounds of the conch, louder than the unheeded, bullying horns of vehicles on the streets, and louder than the voice of light.

This child needed a miracle.

Today, if this silent voice were to win, it might yet save humanity.

Luckily, a garbage collector, an old woman in a yellow saree, noticed her. Ironically, she was deaf; deaf by birth, not by social norms.

The old woman in the yellow saree was revered as something of a saint in the narrow streets of Varanasi. If relatives and friends happened to catch sight of her as they carried the dead body of a loved one on a bamboo bier towards Manikarnika Ghat, they always stopped their chanting of *"Ram Naam Satya Hai"* and bowed low. None was quite sure if they did this out of respect for her, or fear. She was poor, very poor. But she could compete for a spot in the *Forbes Billionaires'* power list—the real power list—because she had it in her to save lives, one at a time. And so, the little girl lying face-down in the dirt, who was destined to fight the world, was rescued by the old woman and taken to the Nameless House with Pink Walls, where she was named "Choti," meaning, simply, "small thing".

It was the early nineteen-eighties, near the Varanasi Ghats.

The River Back Home

New Delhi, 2012

*Wherever you begin, wherever you end,
we all return to the river…*

"Ma'am, but what was the reason? What inspired you go to the Supreme Court to fight this battle, against religion, against society, against ancient customs…?"

"Tell me, what religion teaches differences among people? And anyway, I wasn't fighting *against* anyone, I was fighting *for* someone…"

She watched the short news-clip about her that had been playing on loop throughout the day, followed by the camera cutting to the expert panelists on the show. In a minute, the talk had turned into a slanging match. There was no mention of the injustice done to the widows. Nothing about the extreme life of renunciation they had been condemned to live. Their lives lived in perpetual mourning, not even a spot of color allowed on their person. The argument paid no regard to history, or memory, or fact. It was about nothing. It just was.

The news blared on from the TV in their cramped one-bedroom apartment in north Delhi. The silence in her head began to swell louder than the clamor on TV, until the screaming on the news channel became just so much white noise. Its shrillness penetrated her most silent reaches with its senseless acrimony, unsettling her further.

The front door of their apartment was the color of deep marigold. A garland string of shriveled lemons and green chillies hung atop its worn frame to ward off the evil eye. The living room centered around a small dining table adorned with a vase of plastic sunflowers and had blue walls from which hung many photographs of mother and daughter: graduation pictures, birthday pictures, and all the newspaper clippings of each of her victorious legal cases.

She heard her mother's firm but soothing voice cut through the clamor, at close enough range to become a calming voice-over to her frantic thoughts. "I have packed you some paranthas and mango pickle, dear. And water. Remember, drink plenty of water every day to keep healthy. And don't forget your files," Ma pointed from the kitchen across the room at the pile of legal folders she had left on the table.

She stood, leaning against the bed, in her saree with its pink, fresh-as-the-beginning-of-spring floral print and her light green blouse that offset the leaves of the pattern. When she heard her mother say "file," her heart leapt again and she stared across the room at the dusty brown cardboard folder with the words "Supreme Court Orders" typed out on a manual typewriter.

She was in the bedroom, struggling to fit in the last of her belongings into the old gray polyester duffel bag she always traveled with, but the buzzing noise inside had paralyzed her. Any real arguments and issues that might otherwise have emanated from the TV were rendered insignificant by the acrimonious bluster created by the panel of talking heads. One moment's insignificant gnat of an issue abruptly became the next moment's roiling Pacific Ocean.

"*Beta!* Child, are you listening to me?" Ma said, louder.

She picked up the remote and snapped off the TV, then went back to packing her things, pretending not to hear her mother.

"Why did do you do that?" Ma said, tossing the edge of her pashmina shawl lightly over her Punjabi suit, as she walked up to her.

"Ma, it's just a bunch of nonsense," she said. "It drives me mad."

Ma nodded. "I was watching the evening news and had to listen to that politician Ramchandra and his supporters stave off all charges against him again. I know you are working to bring him to justice, but I am really frightened that you are standing up too tall against these corrupt, powerful goons. It doesn't give me a good feeling."

Standing amidst what felt like all the possessions she owned in the world, now somehow neatly contained on the floor and bed, she turned to her mother. "Amma, you know I have no choice. It's my sworn duty," she said.

Ma's eyes filled with tears as she stepped out onto the small balcony where the setting sun gently soaked the walls in lingering shadows, creating shapes that always seemed to her to be trying to tell her something. At twilight, Ma's west-facing kitchen always glowed with a grayish-orange and muted-blue aura, one that subtly changed depending on the season. Even the smallest of their windows captured the last glowing rays of the sun.

In her mind, she kept hearing the daily chant Ma deployed to make her ever cautious about her job. *Dangerous, very dangerous, dangerous, very dangerous, stay away from criminals, culprits, and corruption…* Ma would even call her at office to chant her lecturing mantra over the phone. She had, guiltily, started putting her mother's calls on mute. Of course, when Ma delivered her lectures in person, she couldn't possibly ignore her.

She became deeply aware of the concern in her mother's face. Every new wrinkle under her eyes, every new gray hair rising from the side of her head, and every changing contour of her face, pressed their concern into her heart.

"Back when I was a journalist, there was much more accountability than there is today. We actually had to get to the root of issues, not just entice people with them like fast food and—" Ma began her most-repeated mantra, and she grinned as she cheekily cut in, "—We have to bring on the revolution by revealing the truth, *not* by seeking ratings."

She laughed as her mother hovered the flat of her hand near her face in a mock slap at her darling child's impertinence, and followed her into the kitchen, inhaling the cloud of steam rising from the pot of masala chai she was brewing with crushed cardamom. The aroma made her feel safe and somehow healed of her worries. Ever since the day she and her colleagues had won the precedent-setting landmark case, her anxiety about what lay ahead had been greatly comforted by Ma's simple daily cooking ritual.

As Ma stood stirring the tea, peering into the pot, she reached around her mother's waist and embraced her from behind burying her face into the older woman's shoulder.

Ma turned and held her face in her hands as she had since she was a little girl. "I could always come with you, child," she said. "We've worked all our lives for this moment. I've been there with you before. Let me come, child, just to be close at hand in case it gets too dangerous for you."

"Ma, it's you who has prepared me every day just for this one day. You are with me every moment," she said.

She'd had this discussion with her mother at least a hundred times, ever since she had won the case. "Ma, we won because of you. You were the one who nurtured the truth, strength, and dignity in me to fight for people's rights. It was you who made this day possible after fighting for years in the Supreme Court in Delhi. Now we are ready to face Ganga Ma. We have kept our promise."

When Ma lowered her eyes, she thought she saw the sheen of tears.

Her trip to Varanasi, her lost and tender Varanasi, the Varanasi of her childhood, was all planned now. This time she had to do it alone. She recalled the moment when she had proudly extended her left hand, palm-up, to receive the Supreme Court's order amid the exuberant, relieved cheers of the crowd and suddenly heard the presiding judge's voice boom: "Everything auspicious is received with both hands." Immediately, she'd thrust both her hands out to receive it.

Reliving the heady excitement of that auspicious moment sent her thoughts momentarily away from Ma's warm graces and the aroma of chai and she walked out of the kitchen and over to the living room table, where she again used both hands to pick up the file before placing it respectfully, reverentially, into her jute shoulder bag.

Ma carried the pot of chai over to the window-sill for their daily ritual, a ritual she would sorely miss. She followed the fragrance like a hummingbird seeks nectar and watched her mother pour the steaming chai in her favorite brass glasses that had beautiful elephants in the pattern of a moon crescent etched along the rim.

"*Pshh*, I am forgetting everything today." Ma got up abruptly and came back carrying some almonds and two Parle-G biscuits—the world's largest-selling biscuit, its Indian manufacturers claimed. Apparently, the "G" in the "Parle-G" stamped large in the center of each biscuit stood for "genius." Perhaps, by feeding her daughter those most popular, quite bland, biscuits every day—(they tasted a bit like sawdust to her!)—Ma had fondly nurtured that hope for her child too.

"Ma, you have to stop feeding me almonds all the time, it's *your* brain that needs them more."

Ma grinned back at her. After a while she said, "When you return, I will make you Varanasi aloo samosas." She smiled, tilting her head and stretching her eyes to indicate how delicious they were. "Will you eat them?"

She looked down into her frothy cup of chai and silently nodded. She felt Ma's warm gaze wash over her in waves.

"Beti, you have matured into a successful adult woman. For this, especially for how far you've had to come, I thank God and ask for His forgiveness every day."

She offered the same exasperated reply she always did: "Ma, you have hundreds of gods, but which one is for forgiveness and which one for thanks?"

She drained her cup of chai and stood up. "I have to leave or else I will miss my train," she said firmly as she turned toward the door. Ma rushed into the kitchen and returned with one hand in a fist and the other held behind her back. Her mother pressed a piece of *mishri*, a small sugar-like rock candy, into her palm and she immediately placed it in her mouth savoring its bitingly sweet flavor. "Happy Birthday, darling" her mother said, smiling. "You know it's Holi tomorrow, the day of your birth."

Holi was a holiday Ma and she could never forget. It was the day of her birth, *and* rebirth. The day the festival of Holi falls each year is determined by the lunar calendar, and Ma and would always wait for that day, whatever the actual date, to celebrate her birthday.

Ma sighed and looked at her. "Beti, you really don't have to go back out into that world, you know. It's very dangerous. You've done enough. The police, politicians, and the local people of Varanasi can take care of this. They've already received copies of the court order."

She looked down, "Ma, I have to go, there are so many things to do, so much that remains unfinished…"

Ma nodded her acceptance and, smiling, handed her the gift she held behind her back. "Here, keep this… when your unfinished work is completed wear this and float a *diya*, an earthen lamp, on the waters of Ma Ganga for me."

"But, but…Ma, I can't take this from you," she said, folding the saree and handing it back to her. It was Ma's favorite saree. Ma had bought it from the shop on the banks of Varanasi. She had worn it on every special occasion—the day she received her adoption papers; the day of her first day at school; the day she passed tenth grade; the day she got her law degree; and, most recently, when she'd won the Supreme Court case of non-discrimination against transgenders and widows in Indian society.

To her, every occasion Ma wore that saree *became* an auspicious one.

Ma's steely look made her hastily rethink her offer. It was the most important occasion of their lives for the *both* of them. Little superstitions such as deciding to accept your mother's favorite saree sometimes seemed to work, even if all they did was to create a subtle aura of positive energy. Ma pressed the saree into her hands and this time she accepted it immediately, holding it against herself and admiring herself in the purple plastic-framed mirror, which bore the marks of leftover adhesive from every one of Ma's stick-on *bindis*—the sparkling jewel-like dots that have adorned Indian women's foreheads since Vedic times; a symbol of consciousness, a symbol of the third eye.

She smiled to herself recalling how she used to tease Ma saying that the red dot on her forehead simply indicated that the "record" button was on, and therefore everything she said was being recorded.

She gave her mother a tight hug and walked out of the door armed with her luggage, her files, the food packets Ma had supplied her with, and the sweetest, warmest memories of the brave woman reporter who had adopted a ten-year-old orphan and changed the course of her life forever.

At the New Delhi Railway Station, she hurriedly jumped out of the auto-rickshaw, unloaded her luggage and rechecked her jute bag. The bustling energy of the Indian capital's train station manifested an amazing irony—one rushed to get to these transit hubs, and then one rushed even more to leave them, almost as if the stations themselves never existed. And once a person left, they never seemed to look back, as if the transition from here-to-there or there-to-here that occurred in these containers of rushing motion barely symbolized a thing.

Her platform was at the farthest end of the station and she ran all the way to her train and coach, checking her ticket for her seat number. She read the ticket once more before hopping on: *Shiv-Ganga Express. Train No. 12559. Dept: ND Railway Station: 18:55.*

As she pushed past the crowds of people in the train, all pilgrims who were going to Varanasi for a dip in the waters of the Ganga, her eyes met those of an elderly woman wearing a pure white saree with the *pallu*, the free edge of the saree, draped over her head.

The woman smiled at her and asked, "Are you from Varanasi?"

"Yes."

"I'm truly blessed to be going to Varanasi too. I've heard people say that Ganga Ma doesn't look as beautiful anywhere as she does there ..." the old woman said wistfully.

She smiled back. Immediately a vision rose in her mind: *a little girl, her body baked nut brown by the sun, lying on her back in a creaky wooden boat, trailing her fingers in a wide, vast river of sun-dappled green-gray, catching the petals of a marigold flower that floated on this majestic confluence of three rivers; by her side was a small mongrel with eyes like melting toffee, and squatting on the helm of the boat, his body wet from diving in for the coins that bereaved families tossed into the auspicious waters to protect their dead, was her best friend...*

She pulled out the food packet Ma had packed her. Though comfortable on her lower berth, she barely closed her eyes all night, too anxious to sleep, mulling over everything that had happened so far, thinking of it over and over till everything dissolved into nothing, and nothing exploded back into everything.

The long sleepless night ended with her staring blankly out of the window at the passing landscape for signs of her eventual destination.

Morning came, and with that the first rays of light peeking above the horizon. She sat up and took in the fact that today was her birthday, it was Holi, and she was back in the town where it had all begun.

THE RIVER BACK HOME

At last she finally saw the name that she had so far only imagined seeing at each of the previous four stations: It was only a sign, but to her it was akin to a tourist finally visiting the Taj Mahal after seeing pictures of it everywhere, in books, postcards, tourist brochures, movies, posters, advertisements—so familiar that though this was the first time one was actually seeing it, it felt as if one had been there many times before. Seeing the Varanasi sign caused a similar effect in her—the difference was the sign was exactly as she had left it, exactly as she had *actually* seen it twenty years ago to the day, and had seen it since in her dreams every night.

"Varanasi Junction" The town's name appeared on an iron signboard in bold letters emblazoned across a background that shimmered as bright and yellow as the summer sun at its peak. It was written in English, Hindi, and Urdu. Varanasi, it was a Sanskrit name derived from the name of the rivers Varuna and Asi, between which the city was built, a naked city where the truth had nothing to hide beneath, no modesty cloth, no veil; a city where you felt so close to death that you were always aware of being alive. How ironic that the "City of the Dead" was the oldest living city in human civilization.

The train lurched through a cloud of its own smoke to a stop.

She had reached her destination.

She grabbed her belongings and made her way deftly through the chaotic throng of passengers filing out of the train's narrow crowded corridors. When she finally set her feet on the platform it was as if the ground seemed to tug at her entire being with the familiarity of an old friend. Her eyes sought her shadow that stretched long and transparent, like a tangle of film, across Varanasi Station's stout asymmetrical iron pillars that had been painted and re-painted an endless number of times and now stood rusting. *How*, she wondered, *can anything seem so newly painted from a distance while a closer look reflected only the crumbling rust and decay of an epic struggle for survival?*

The jagged zigzag of torn signs and posters that adorned the station's walls seemed to have been artfully organized to fill the space. The walls were a fading yellow, coated with paint that was somewhere smooth and seamless and in other places peeling so markedly as to reveal the naked bricks behind that had been fired and stacked into a station wall more than a century ago. The sun hung at about the same position as her height, the same now as it was then.

Were the shadows encroaching again? Those dark sights, sounds, and scents of the memories I thought I had eclipsed more than twenty years ago?

She rummaged for her phone and called Ma. Her mother picked up even before the phone completed one ring. Ma always had a sixth sense about her, one she could never hope to evade, and really, why would she ever want to? She imagined her mother, still sitting at the windowsill, waiting for her with two cups of masala chai—like she had always waited, every evening since she had returned to Delhi after graduating from Law School in Mumbai. Her simple ritual with the cups of chai, she knew, was what made her mother feel as if she was always near, whether or not she was actually there to drink the tea or inhale its fragrant aroma.

"Beti? Are you safe?" Her mother answered the phone breathlessly.

"Ma, I'm on the platform at Varanasi. I've made it. Relax."

"Oh! Bless you, my child, happy birthday my golden one, happy Holi, may god grant you a thousand years of life! Please take care of yourself. Beti, I can't tell you how happy I am you've reached the end of your long journey. *Rab Rakha tera. Jeeti Reh, Khush Reh*, God will look after you, a long happy life to you, always."

It wasn't just the natural freshness of morning or the spring-bound energy of impending summer, it wasn't the marigold-seller and his fragrant wares or the slight moisture that caressed the air, it wasn't anything her mind could grasp or her hands could hold, it was just Varanasi that impelled her feet lightly forward on their own so that she was almost skipping.

She entered the city in a dream, ignoring the hawkers and the coolies, her free hand lightly grazing the hundreds of colored imprints of joyous, outstretched hands on the painted and repainted wall. Then she heard a soft distant chiming sound that grew louder and more reminiscent of a voice, and it caused her to stop. She had forgotten about this chiming sound for years, but clearly it had survived and now echoed along Varanasi's narrow sun-less streets.

"*Choti! Chotiiii, run!*"

She whirled around! Her eyes searched every corner!

Though the city was filled to the brim with its own people and Holi visitors, plus their hundreds of thousands of pigmented hands of every shape and social standing, there was no one she recognized.

She saw a group of kids playing with the colors of Holi. She started walking again when one of them, dressed as Durga—the beatific, many-armed Hindu warrior-goddess whose mission it is to defend dharma against evil—approached to stand in front of her. The micro-goddess and she stared at each other, and then she smiled at her. The little girl smiled back and shyly put a smear of red color on her cheek.

Varanasi was the kind of place whose colorful, spiritual energy could be detected with one's eyes closed, just from inhaling its air, and she was breathing in all of that air again. Varanasi's chaos was the chaos called "life," and the town's beautiful chaotic life swirled eternally amid its winding streets and temples down to the very banks of the Ganga river.

The chaos of that day had particularly vibrant hues due to it being the start of Holi. Street carts and vendors appeared everywhere, loaded with piles and small packs of powder, the many-colored powders from indigo to vermilion to yellow to rani-pink, all to be joyously tossed around and smeared on faces all day and all-night long. Yellow-like-turmeric or red-like-chilli, they were all on display, ready to explode.

Varanasi had barely blinked her beautiful eyes awake, yet already more and more groups of buoyant children were coming out of every corner, playing with colors, tossing the powdered pigment high above their heads and at each other, creating haphazard rainbows and atmospheres. She imagined what the scene would be like if a typhoon were to suddenly appear—the entire town would be swept away, yes, but swept away in the most joyous colors!

A little further, what seemed to be the city's entire population began to run past her, racing to reach the legendary corner wall at the turn to *Bhoot Gali,* Ghost Alley, and imprint it with their color-soaked hands. She paused to stand by her favorite wall, which had probably been painted many times after she had left this town. Blue like a peacock's neck, yellow like marigold, red like a nightingale's eyes, pink like the color of a Rajasthani woman's saree on Teej celebration—handprints of every hue and dimension stamped atop, covering the wall.

Another group of children dressed as Hindu gods and goddesses passed by, some as Krishna, some as Parvati, some as Rama, and the last one as Shiva, his tiny body painted the blue that signifies immortality, who bolted to the wall of hands, then turned back to toss a handful of powder—a color-burst of dusky rose hit her cheek—as if seeking to highlight something on a blank page. Instinctively, she covered her handbag with her arms, tightened her grip on her jute shoulder bag, covering it with her saree, and picked up her pace.

She finally stopped at a street corner, where the ancient branches and roots of an old banyan tree had long prised apart the abandoned Hanuman temple in the corner of the crossroads, which, doubtless, must have once had a glorious past. Though the temple was deserted, nature had embraced it in its arms, laying bare its ruins with the roots of a tree, as if to reveal a more gut-wrenchingly honest story about its genesis than its formerly solidly plastered and painted walls.

She spied a broken concrete bench across from the tree's conquest, and crossed the road to sit there for a moment to admire the steady, yearning power of nature. For more good luck, she picked up a pebble and tucked it into her bag next to the Supreme Court orders. She never really understood the human desire to cherish pebbles, yet here she was indulging it. Did this strange desire, this natural whim, reach back to prehistoric times when our ancestors might have played with such small stones, or used them as tools, or collected them as souvenirs of the earth itself, perhaps out of some prescient instinct that the earth would someday disappear; or simply because they considered them inherently auspicious. The mystery of pebbles.

It had been twenty years since she had last walked these Varanasi streets on Holi. They appeared to her like Indradhanush or the bow of Indra the Sun God or a rainbow having descended to earth. Nothing seemed familiar, yet she didn't need to ask anyone for directions because even with no real cognizance, she trusted her legs, in their determination, stride, speed, and confident turns, to take her where she needed to go.

She emerged out of the tiny tentacle of an alley, onto a small lane without any identity, any sign, or even a name, onto Bhoot Gali.

Two decrepit ancient structures alongside two jarringly modern ones, and she arrived at her destination.

Cars crowded the streets and sidewalks, sacred cows wandered around or stopped to stare and chew, Holi celebrants gathered in groups with their powders, and thin rickshaw-pullers struggled through the morning rush.

She had her own struggle to make as she lugged her bags through the sun-deprived streets toward the ashram of her memory, stopping at a low, ornate, but rusted metal gate, and looked across at the dilapidated courtyard it haplessly sought to protect.

In the corner of the courtyard, next to the now crumbling wall, towered a huge mango tree. The grass around its sturdy trunk, which struck her as more like that of a huge elephant's than a tree's, had turned brown in patches. Exactly thirty-three steps—she had once counted them—from the trunk of the mango tree stood the ashram, its once white facade now dull and yellowed. After retracing her steps of years' ago with her eyes, she reached out and pushed open the gate. As it creaked open, she felt the dam of her mind restrain the flood of images that wanted to overrun it. *A loud voice, the same chiming one as before, soared across her ears, "Choti! Run! Run and never look back!"*

She stood rooted in exactly the same spot as she had then, at the same gate, but back when it would have been freshly painted at the slightest scuff or trace of dirt or rust.

The courtyard had been different then, with soothing beds of holy basil and tulsi populating its center, and without such a sprawling mango tree. Now, though the ashram had decayed, the plants remained, but barely. In her memory, the ashram, though it was no longer that way, would always be white, new, young, and welcoming as a heavenly garden.

Across the courtyard near the ashram, in the partial shadow of the mango tree, her colleagues Alka and Geeta, who had arrived the night before to ensure that the ashram was secure and that the local police had been informed of today's celebrations, were deep in conversation. Before this day, neither the police nor the locals would have spared a thought for the old crumbling ashram. Like its inmates, it too had almost been invisible—colorless for decades.

The winds of change had finally enveloped this sacred space.

The news of Holi being played by color-deprived widows had spread and grabbed everyone's attention. Sometimes a war between the new and the old wants to erupt in ancient cities, but many want to abort the revolution before it is born. Ancient cities have witnessed war, disaster, and conflict, yet sometimes change seems like their most threatening enemy. An unchanging, unquestioning society is the safest way to preserve the status quo. But who wanted safety for some and oppression for others? *She* certainly didn't.

Her greatest fear was that all of Varanasi, maybe all of India, might resist, or burst into sudden conflict upon witnessing the change of ideals, ideas, laws, and customs to come. No matter; she had come too far not to be there to protect the new, while fending off the old. She had to be there to help greet the dawn of a new Holi, whose rays could be enjoyed by all.

She quietly entered through the gate and stood near the tulsi plant that was planted in an ornate but cracked iron pot set on a podium. Seeing the dry tulsi struggling to raise its branches past the rim of the broken pot, she thought how this plant—which had once been so cared for and loved, and by someone who was so dedicated to it—had no choice but to shrivel after time and circumstance had caused that love to disappear.

Without love, not even a tulsi plant can survive.

A throng of women in white sarees sat in the courtyard, their backs resting against the crumbling walls of the ashram, carrying the burden of their own worn, staring, somber faces; faces she was almost respectfully ashamed to look at. These plain women, enshrouded in unavoidable, unforgiving white, were India's widows. White was their color of mourning, and these women were expected, as per Hindu custom, to remain for the rest of their lives in this perpetual state of mourning.

Why? She knew why, but she could never accept the answer.

Indian widows were considered inauspicious; having outlived their husbands they were nothing but a burden on their families; society had no use for them and so used religion as a means of marginalizing them. They were banished far away from their homes and told to live a life of complete abstinence, to eke out the rest of their existence, to emaciate themselves, to live on the bare minimum.

Since India's ancient times, many still believed that color is what made women beautiful, more young and vibrant, and therefore, more desirable. No doubt some overly superstitious someone in our long history must have wanted the widows, in their perceived absence of desirability, to look destitute and isolated and plain, and the easiest way was to take all traces of color away from them.

As she reverentially circumambulated the tulsi, the widows who had gathered in the courtyard eyed her with some amount of suspicion. Most of them, courtesy of Alka and Geeta, likely knew that she was the attorney with "the file."

After completing her circle (and making the silent wish that even this shriveling tulsi would one day return to its full lush and green glory), she took those self-same thirty-three steps she had in the past toward the mango tree. She had always loved the fresh scent of mango leaves, and this time it was mixed with a scent of roses that had wafted in from somewhere.

She traced the rose scent back to one side of the courtyard where several widows were tearing petals from a heap of roses and scattering them into a beautiful rich pink carpet. The sight was impressive, even more so, admittedly, against the backdrop of the widows' oppressive white sarees. To see widows actually touching colorful rose petals almost brought tears to her eyes.

As if with a mind of their own, her feet lead her to the mango tree. She climbed up a low brick wall and leaned into its branches to smell a tiny unripe mango. She breathed in deeply.

It smelled like childhood itself.

As she inhaled the unripe mango's scent, she swiveled her head to look for a particular far corner in the wall. There, as if it had been waiting for someone to find it before it decayed with time, clung a small strand of plastic peeking out from a crack in the bricks, a strand so small that only someone who knew it was there could have found it.

She lowered herself to the ground, and reached her arm elbow-deep into the gap in the bricks until her fingers felt a familiar crevice—their secret hiding place. She pulled out a plastic-wrapped, yellowing, dog-eared notebook that, literally, when she touched it, made her body shake. She was shaking so much, she had to glance back to make sure she wasn't causing the widows to suspect her even more.

She pulled the long-hidden bundle out, pulled off the plastic wrap with trembling fingers, opened it to the first page, and traced the first line with her finger. It said, "*Meri Choti, Mera Chand,*" in Hindi.

The simple line almost exploded the floodgates she had erected around her heart. The word "*meri*" is a small one, but it's a word with the potential to change the course of the universe. Meri means "mine". The idea that she had belonged to someone suddenly broke her heart. Someone who had once told her when she was young, "Never give pet names to stray dogs, they won't leave you, and will follow you till death."

This profound feeling shook every last inch of professional resistance from her body and she slumped to the bottom of the wall sobbing like the little girl she once had been.

In her vision, she saw her face, through her tears she saw Ganga, then into her heart entered her namesake, the one whose name she had chosen as her own: *Noor*.

"Someone, get this young woman some water."

"Daughter, are you okay?"

"What happened? What happened to her?"

Her suddenly overwhelmed behavior—and she was the lawyer come to help *them*—soon grabbed everyone's attention, and threatened to cause the gathering of local women who were supporting the Holi celebrations for the widows, to surround her and embrace her personal turmoil and turn it into a public one, when it was *their* turmoil that mattered most. The women's concerned voices fell around her like a protective cover.

Alka saw the open notebook she had dropped in her lap and lifted it to her face. "Who is this Choti?" she asked, after reading the line that had sent her crashing to the earth.

She sipped at the cup of water one of the widows had handed her and sighed deeply. All she could do was look at Alka's concerned face, then trace her stare as it became lost in the ashram's faded white balcony above, which now seemed to rise as high as heaven itself...

Tamasha

Varanasi, 1992

*A fine balance between stage and life:
both replicating each other*

"*Aawa-aawa paisa kamawa
Ek lagawa du kamawa
Du lagawa char kamawa
Kuch na lagawa
Ghantta hilawa
Aawa-aawa bhaiya aawa
Bhauji ke bhi saath le aawa*"

"Come, come; earn a sum,
Make two on bidding one,
Make four on bidding two,
Stay a zero by bidding none
Come come, brother come,
Bring your wife too; earn a sum!"

Chintu's raucous singing had gathered a ragtag crowd that had assembled to watch the miracle of Choti walking above them on her tight-rope. She was dressed in her favorite yellow frock with the black polka dots and carrying the balancing pole that her friend and partner Chintu had made for her. She had found the dress at Manikarnika Ghat, the steps where people cremated their loved ones, and often discarded their deceased's favorite possessions. Manikarnika was where she found most of her treasures. Chintu, had set up the bamboo tripod from which the rope was strung and was now trying to get the people to pay to watch the performance.

Choti had known Chintu all her life, or at least as far back as she could remember. They had both been "raised" in the Nameless House with Pink Walls and now, at the age of about eleven, they both worked with each other, annoyed each other, played with each other, fought with each other—but always had each other's backs if a *third* person tried to mess with them. Some of the other children used to say that their names should be "Shiv" and "Parvati." That kind of made sense, for those were the gods they always dressed as, every year on Shivrathri, the festival of Lord Shiv. They made a lot of money on this day. Choti was happy enough being Parvati to Chintu's Shiv, but got really mad when he did not share the money they made together, fair and square. Then they had the most awful fights!

What Chintu and she had was a love-hate, lost-found, earned-stolen, sweet-salty relationship.

They usually set up their small act near the Tulsi Ghat, the great amphitheater-like steps that led down to River Ganga. It was the safest place for Chintu and Choti to set up their *tamasha*, their performance, because it was easy to escape from here when the police inevitably arrived to break up their ring of admirers, some of whom would give them a few rupees in exchange for their efforts.

The narrow streets behind Tulsi Ghat were like a huge maze so it was easy to disappear into them to avoid being caught in the ensuing chase. Chintu always joked that it wasn't so much the maze they fled into that made it hard for the cops to catch them, but the cops' potbellies and weak lungs, that had them huffing and puffing in no time.

That day, three people had bet against Choti, putting their money in Chintu's battered cap—the one with a check-mark on it that he'd been given by a tourist—hoping to double their money if she fell off the tight-rope before Round three.

Choti had completed the first round, walking carefully back and forth along the rope with the balancing stick and afterwards everyone had applauded. As she readied for Round two, the first money-collecting round, Chintu raised his voice above the crowd's din and announced: "One rupee, two rupees, three rupees. The tamasha is on! All you have to do is pay and you can see more."

One of the men shouted: "We're fed up with the old tricks, show us something new…"

"Okay, place a bet and earn three times what you put in," Chintu offered.

"No, tell the girl to walk without her balancing stick," the man said, upping the challenge.

Chintu hesitated, then turned to Choti with false bravado in his voice: "*Aiy*, Choti, toss that pole away…"

Choti was indignant, stuck one arm on her waist and gesticulated at him with the other: "Oh, *really*? And what if

I fall? *I'll* be the one to break my limbs; what do you stand to lose?"

Chintu looked at her square in the eyes. Then he made the V-sign with two fingers pointing first at his own eyes, then towards Choti's as if to say, "I'm watching you." It was the sign he always made to give her confidence. But under his breath he muttered, *"If you fall, I'll lose my life…"*

Choti rolled her eyes in exasperation. She loved performing this act. It made her feel that people were paying to see a bird fly, defying gravity. But the gambling was another matter. It gave her a strange feeling. She felt sympathy for the people who lost their money but she felt worse for those who won, because they didn't have to earn or work hard for the cash the way she did.

She put a foot forward, tottered, and immediately stepped back on the platform.

"*Bakwas* act, total rubbish, she will surely fall before taking two steps!" the man who had placed a bet said dismissively, looking all around for support.

"She will fall before she walks even half the rope," another guy said, laughing like a lunatic.

Choti looked down at the top of their heads from the platform's edge. It was like looking down on a dark, swaying forest from above. "I'll show you, I'll walk the full rope, and with no balancing stick. How many steps can you walk up here, you fat man?" she screamed back.

Chintu, keeping one eye on the growing pile of rupees in his cap, yelled over the crowd, "Choti, just focus." Choti craved Chintu's confidence even though at other times she almost believed she could walk on the clouds if she set her mind to it.

Standing on the platform, she wound her long unruly hair into a knot and set her first step on the rope, balancing her body by counterbalancing her arms. As Choti took her first step, Chintu's lower lip began to wobble uncontrollably. This always happened to him when he was nervous and it almost always caused Choti's lip to tremble too. Chintu was such an idiot, she thought. She was already a nervous wreck after no one had bet that she would complete her walk without the balancing stick. How could she concentrate if he was worried too?

As she tried to calm her lip with her tongue, she wondered why most people would rather hope for others to fail than hope for them to succeed. So few are eager to imagine that the other might fly, or in her case, walk without her stick. She looked straight ahead and imagined herself suddenly taking off like a baby bird learning to fly.

Then came what was always her favorite moment: when she felt like she had *actual* wings and had broken the bond of gravity. Defying the dark pull of gravity, she came into perfect balance after taking three assertive steps, and then like a dancer slowly crossed the half-rope mark. Satisfied, she looked down briefly to absorb the aura of the Ganga washing over her, while beaming her triumph at all those who had bet she would fall, especially that screaming lunatic.

The money was secondary to the high rope-walking gave her, but still she kept one eye (and sometimes her third-eye) on Chintu, as he gathered their pile of winnings, into his battered cap.

The excitement had built and come to a peak, and she lived for being the center of its attention. Choti felt she could do anything up in the air. Being at that height made her feel superior to everyone else on earth, while not much else did, and that alone made her feel free.

Because she was the one highest up, she also had to serve as the lookout for the cops. Sure enough, there they came, charging and bumbling, potbellies and all, down Tulsi Ghat's steps to break up their tamasha. She had almost arrived at the far platform when she first saw them, and seeing them, almost burst her lungs as she stumbled, shouting, "Run! Police!"

The crowd dispersed, and she jumped off the rope and began to run too, but she wasn't running from the cops—she was running to catch Chintu! Every time after the cops came to break up their tamasha, he tucked "their" rupees atop his head under his cap, and tried to cheat Choti by racing away with all the money before she could even reach the ground. That day, she was determined to catch her thief of a partner.

She raced up the steps and caught a fleeting glimpse of him as he disappeared into the maze of streets. "Chintu, you thug! When I catch you, I will kill you. Last year you lost all our savings in gambling and I couldn't go to school! I won't let you do it this time," she shrieked as she quickened her pace after him. "And if you steal or spend the money I earned for us and risked my life for, I will cremate you alive at Manikarnika Ghat, I swear!"

Choti was fast, but Chintu could run much faster than her—since they had started their tamasha racket, he had to learn to run fast just so she wouldn't try to kill him every time for stealing her money. Choti passed a tour guide as she ran and overheard him telling a pilgrim about Varanasi, "This is the oldest living city of the dead. Nothing can hide in this city, not life, not death, nothing, it's all out in the open for you to see."

What the guide said was true. In Varanasi, amid its colors, chaos, and semi-organized rabble, life and death coexisted, and it was all naked to the eye. Truth and inevitability were neither hidden nor distant. Both existed between the smoke and the bells, between the shades of flame and ash, between the funeral pyres and the healing, blessed, holy river. There was nothing to chase in Varanasi. It was its own chase and its own final place of rest, where all egos, possessions, disputes, secrets, time, space, light, dark, spirits, and materials could be peacefully and uncontroversially placed on a pyre to meet a Ganga-borne end.

In this oldest surviving city of the dead, the chaser was bound to be chased; the buyer bound to be sold; a river bound to quench its thirst; and she was bound to chase Chintu for the meager rupees she had earned, unaffected by the constant parade of burning bodies or moksha-seeking pilgrims.

Choti had always hated Manikarnika and its screaming tea-stall hawkers, misers who saved every penny, the confection-making *halwais* with their protruding stomachs, the wealthy women with their golden bangles, the self-entitled men with their fancy cars, and their broods of self-entitled children—no one from any caste could escape this ghat. What differentiated Varanasi from any other place in the world was that on one side of the banks people prayed for immortality and wealth, while on the other, their loved ones were slowly fed to the fire, leaving all their wealth behind.

Choti braced herself and then continued her chase past the many tea-stalls and breakfast-kiosks situated precariously on the uneven steps leading down to the water, cutting through the ebb and flow of disoriented tourists, pilgrims, and bewildered schoolkids. She was so determined to catch Chintu, she even passed under the many biers, the movable stretchers designed to carry the deceased to their funerals via coffin or cremation. Carrying the deceased bodies of loved or not-so-loved ones to the Ganga on these biers is an ancient tradition. The biers are adorned with colorful pennants and shining paper buntings when one has lived a complete life, and dressed in old whites or faded rags when someone has lived an accursed one.

Suddenly an old man, an old Manikarnika guard, grabbed her arm right outside the last gate through which she saw Chintu running away with her money. The guard's eyes were yellow and oozing, and he tried to shoo her off, back in the direction she had come, with wild motions of his dirty hands. "You! You get out, you get out of here! Girls can't be here."

Chintu had hoodwinked her again! She kept thinking about the conversation they had had two nights ago, lying in the dry leaves beneath the old banyan tree:

"Chintu, yaar, I don't want us to be scavengers like the other streetkids. I want us want to live in real homes and go to school. Remember, how we both stood outside the school wall to learn the National Anthem that day?"

"I'll put you in school someday, Choti don't worry. *Mein hoon na?* I'm there for you, aren't I?" Chintu had replied. "Besides, I'm going to grow up and be a cop and beat those potbellies black and blue…"

"I'll be the *chief* of the cops and beat you for stealing all my money," Choti had said dismissing her partner with a toss of her head.

If Chintu didn't believe in change, then neither would I, she had thought then. But the truth was that she just loved the uniforms the kids wore at that school, the bags and tiffins they came with. Most of all she like watching their parents, when they came to fetch them at the school gates. How tightly the kids held their parents' hands. How sweetly the mummys smiled.

Chintu was less enamored. He claimed that to him a uniform was silly; it was like being put into a cloning machine.

It was humiliating to be kept out of the Manikarnika Ghats, but every time she laid eyes or set foot there her spirit became paralyzed anyway, so what did it matter? She had not yet lost anyone. But then she never had anyone to lose, and so had never understood the pain. She only snuck into Manikarnika Ghat to pilfer the belongings left by the deceased or to help her orphaned housemates sieve the ashes of the deceased's cremated skulls for their gold fillings.

Most people in Varanasi referred to the scavenging kids as "rodents" or "sewage dwellers," but all the orphans considered themselves the reincarnations of gods and goddesses. All of them had one thing in common: every day, they woke up expecting some sort of magic to happen, like the overnight metamorphosis of a caterpillar into a butterfly. But in the world outside, the reality of things was very different. No one trusted them because they had neither a name nor a home. There were no Cinderella stories they could hope for, because no palaces were open to them.

Some kids from the Nameless House with Pink Walls became beggars, some worked as daily laborers, some dressed up as gods and goddesses, and some scavenged and sold the ornaments left by the deceased. She was the only tight-rope-walker among the bunch, and, up until then, Chintu had helped her with her act.

Choti finally managed to evade the guard and enter the ghat. After she had tiptoed past the burning bodies and piles of smoldering ash and made it to the shore, she was so out of breath and thirsty that she sucked water from the first leaking tap she found.

As she stepped back, she suffered the bad fortune of stepping into a steaming fresh pile of pungent cowdung. "*Oh Teri!*" she squealed.

Cows may have been sacred, but at that moment, she had other beliefs about their dung! Chintu, gripping his cap tight to his head so as not to lose the rupees he had won, heard her loud swear and turned around to see the mess she had stepped into.

"Ha ha ha! Happy Baarrrday, Choti!" she looked at the holy Ganga and whom did she see but Chintu drifting away in a boat! He even had the gall to lift his stupid check-mark cap, grin, and wave the small wad of notes he had stolen from her.

"Chintu! You bloody loser!" she shrieked. "Next it will be your turn! I'll collect the money and fly away. Or get another assistant! I don't need you! *I'm* the one they come to see." Choti tore at her clothes in frustration and wheeled around through the smoke and pyres to the staircase to inspect her dung-smeared feet.

"Stupid dog, bloody Chintu. Took all my rupees. I'm the one who walks the tight-rope, I'm the one who knows how to fly!" she grumbled aloud to no one, as she sat down on the steps leading down to the river and began stamping and scraping her feet.

A splash of cowdung shaken off her foot went flying into the air!

"Hey, watch it, child," she heard a woman's voice say. "You have no regard for anyone, wretched girl... and such abusive language. You street kids are the worst."

Choti looked up from her smelly feet to see seated beside her an elderly woman draped in a saree as white as the first white blossoms of jasmine. Her saree had flecks of cowdung on it, which she was trying to shake off without actually touching it as she had just come back from a purifying dip at Ma Ganga.

A chai-wallah nearby scowled at Choti too: "I tell you, they're not street kids they're street *scum*. Scavengers. Sewage rats. The lowest of the low. Besides, they're all thieves too… always looking to make off with your stuff…"

Choti scowled at the emaciated old woman. She had a shorn head and, Choti immediately noticed, was reading an ancient-looking book with a pink cover, apparently as old as her, concealed inside a large, hardbound copy of the *Bhagwad Gita*. "Who are you, some kind of schoolteacher Madamji?" she said rudely. And Madamji, what is this inside your holy book? Is it some filmi love story?"

At once the woman looked so scared that Choti felt bad for her. I mean, after all Choti had dirtied her saree, but the woman hadn't hit her or anything. She should have been more respectful to this elder—especially one clever enough to hide one book, whatever it was, inside another so she could read it in peace—but that damn Chintu had got her in a foul mood.

The old lady hid her double book under her saree as Choti ranted on, venting her frustration with Chintu: "*Chor!* Dog! Son of a pig! He stole all of the money I risk my life for every day! I swear, I will burn him alive—just like they do with all these dead people."

"Then, child, you will go to prison," the old lady announced.

Choti looked up to scowl at the woman again; this time she was smiling, amused perhaps at Choti's immense anger. Now that she had set aside her book she was looking at her. It was a gaze of deep, serene understanding; the kind of understanding that can only come from the pain of great sacrifice and loss. Instead of chiding her or telling her she wasn't supposed to be at Manikarnika in the first place because she was a girl, the old woman was teasing her.

Choti stared at her a moment, wanting to say something tough to scare her off, so she said: "Okay then, I won't burn Chintu, I will *drown him*."

The woman smiled again and moved her gaze towards the Ganga. "Angry girl, how do you fight for your food all day long? And who is this Chintu?"

For some reason, Choti found herself opening out to the old woman: "I'm a tight-rope walker. Chintu is my partner, sometimes a cheating dishonest one. We have an all-day tamasha together. We go all day long without a break. If we took a break, we wouldn't survive. I fly and float up in the air, balancing on a rope, and he gathers the crowd, takes their bets, and collects the money we win, after I walk my tight-rope without falling off. Anyway, why do you ask? Are you a teacher who wants to put me in school? I noticed you are not reading your 'holy book' anymore," Choti finished with pointed sarcasm.

"What happened to your feet?" The old lady looked at her filthy legs without answering her question.

"I stepped into a pile of fresh cowdung when I was chasing that shameless thief, and he turned around and screamed, 'Happy Baarrrday', the bloody son of a pig."

The old lady ignored her invective. "I can see your feet are dirty, but what I am asking, child, is about all the cuts and welts on them," she said.

Choti silently lowered her gaze and clasped her calloused hands together, suddenly aware of how dirty she was. She felt embarrassed, but just for a moment.

"They look like the feet of an old, poor, outcast who has no shoes," the old lady said. "And all the cuts and scrapes on your fingers and hands. Are those from the cowdung, too?"

Choti found herself impulsively confiding in the old woman; telling her much more than she normally shared with strangers. "Oh, these are from the rope I set up and walk on, and from the stick I use to balance so I don't fall. Sometimes, when I have to make the rope tighter or grip the stick real hard to balance properly, it cuts into my feet and hands. It's part of my job."

"I see," was all the woman said. She kept staring at her.

"You know, I do tamasha, but somedays I feel that everyone is doing their own tamasha—that stupid old man guarding Manikarnika, who thinks he can guard death itself; the Halwai uncle who claims he can keep my shadow off his food; Chintu, the double-crossing son of a pig, who happens to be my partner—I won't use foul language about him again, I promise, but he is also running his own tamasha, sneaking one tamasha inside another one, sort of like you with your books! I mean, *everyone* has some tamasha or the other." Choti's face was flush with anger.

As she listened to the little girl's rant, the old woman's smile grew longer and sadder. "Girl, I only pray that your feet and hands heal one day," she said finally, then clutching her book within a book close to her chest she picked up the brass pot placed beside her, and hugging her books closer to her chest, started walking down the crooked steps toward the river. She paused on the last step and turned around: "What's your name, daughter?"

"First tell me yours," Choti instantly demanded.

The lady said nothing. For a moment, her mouth tried forming the word as though unused to having said it in a long while, then she changed her mind, turned on her heel and was gone.

Choti didn't let on, but the truth was that she had often seen the old woman around in that area, but it was the first time she had ever spoken to her, and by pure chance. Or was it chance? Could chance simply be another tamasha?

It had been a different old woman, a garbage-collector draped in a soiled yellow saree, who had first rescued Choti and taken her to the "orphanage", the Nameless House with Pink Walls. It was there that she left all the abandoned babies she chanced upon in the garbage or on the streets or near the sewage pipes or in the backyard of hospitals. She was deaf but had a sixth sense about these tiny infants, these little pods of new life in the city of the dead. Only she heard the wail of these infants; it was the only cry she was attuned to hear. She brought them to the Nameless House to rescue them from everything—from crippling shame and insecurity to garbage and rodents.

For a decrepit place open to the sun, the Nameless House remained surprisingly cool, even in the hot summers, cooled by the mist-laden breeze that slipped over the Ganga and comforted the children. The crying infants' brows were soothed by the soft caress of Ma Ganga and lulled back to sleep. The orphans had already overcome thunderstorms of strife by sheer human resilience, an overcoming that often marked them with one disability or another, after which they were then named. If a child had had his toes nibbled off by a rat while still abandoned in the garbage dump, he or she might be called "Three-Toes" or "Four-Toes." One with a broken leg, a missing eye or broken nose, was simply "Half Leg" or "One Eye" or "Noseless" or even just "Kallu" for the dark-skinned ones. Once someone was named, that name was theirs for life.

Chintu was named after Lord Krishna, whose curly hair his baby hair resembled. But when Chintu grew a little older the texture of his hair changed, while his name remained the same. A boy named "Curlyhead" with straight hair. Calling the orphans after their most distinctive feature was absolutely reasonable to the Nameless Owner of the Nameless House with Pink Walls, as otherwise how could he possibly remember all their names? There were just too many of them.

The Nameless House with Pink Walls was really just a dilapidated courtyard protected by a strangely aggressive cow, whose hay shed also served as a shack for some of the orphans, and whose milk nourished the children. A small tulsi altar stood in the middle of the courtyard. Next to the entrance stood a rusted tin can, which had probably been planted there to sell ghee. Many of the rich people who came to Varanasi for moksha and cremation preferred using ghee to light the pyres of their beloved ones.

The Nameless Man who watched over the Nameless House and lived in a small room in the attic he accessed by a wooden ladder, never understood the point of all these rituals—once you were gone, you were gone. He left the ragged urchins to do their business: some of whom worked Manikarnika for whatever they could scrounge, and some of whom begged.

The kids who worked Manikarnika Ghat often returned rich, having retrieved the wondrous treasures that remained after the family members had cremated their loved ones and spread their remains in the Ganga. They jumped into the river looking for gold teeth, rings and personal belongings that might have survived the blaze. Sometimes there were coins that were tossed into the water. On lesser days they returned with clothes, toys and cosmetics.

Choti grew up never quite feeling at home in the Nameless House with Pink Walls, despite its holding the magic of children learning to take care of one another in order to survive. Despite the fact that her best friend, and worst enemy, Chintu lived there too.

The owner, the Nameless Man, had very little to do with them. He was a stranger who, it was rumored, had moved to Varanasi from a very far-away land, whose location no one knew. Some people in the neighborhood even suspected him of being a criminal, a kind of drug-dealer. He didn't care either way. No one really had any idea how he came to dwell in and operate the Nameless

House with Pink Walls, and he was so bold in his position there that whenever government officials came to collect their house tax, he would abuse them, saying, "These are all my children, I am doing God's work here and you want taxes from me? Sin! Sin! Sin! For your greed and aggression, you and your next generations will rot in hell, and any past ones will reappear to torture you." The Nameless Man's bold chiding on behalf of his orphans always worked, and provided one of the only times the children living there heard his gruff voice.

The children grew up as if on their own, sprouting like mushrooms; as if they lived on the planet Mercury, where a year goes by almost four times faster than a year on Earth. The children always had enough to eat—courtesy the relatives of the departed who traveled there, and who tended, out of guilt and fear for their loved ones, to feed the orphans in a last-ditch effort to help the souls of their dearly departed make their Karmic journey.

People from the West, tourists mostly, and the more gentle-hearted residents in the area often came to the Nameless House with Pink Walls for photo-ops. In exchange, the Nameless Man would ask them to donate cash, which he collected in an empty rusted tin with a slit cut into the top.

Once, while she was practising her tight-rope-walking skills near the ghats, Choti thought she saw the Old Woman in a Yellow Saree carrying a child she had rescued from the lapping tides of the Ganga, just like she had with her. Choti waved at her and danced a little twist on her rope to show her gratitude.

The other old lady, Noor, came every day to the same place between the Tulsi Ghat and Manikarnika to collect water from the Ganga to offer the tulsi plant that grew in the courtyard of the widow's ashram, where she had lived for over fifty years. When she returned, she never failed to first water the tulsi with Ganga water before circumambulating it. Like her, the sturdy little plant had been there, in the same pot, in the same place, for as far as she could remember.

That day too, after watering the tulsi, Noor floated to the rear of the courtyard and sat on its red terracotta tiles, glancing around to make sure none of the other widows were watching—they loved to gossip—as she took the pink-wrapped book out of the *Bhagavad Gita* and carefully wrapped it in the scrap of plastic she had found on her way back from the Ganga. She rose to her feet, and counted her steps as she approached the newly planted mango tree. Beside the mango was a brick wall. Noor approached the wall, found a gap in the bricks near its corner, and secretly tucked her pink book within.

When Noor crept back from the corner, she spied the dozen or so other white-enshrouded women spilling onto the courtyard, plain white rice filling their steel mealtime plates. She watched as the group of widows sat on the floor and began to eat, then went into the ashram to get her own plate of rice, returning with it to sit among the other women. Noor ate her small mound of rice grain by grain. As she ate, the deeply soothing voice of a venerable old man, speaking deeply soothing words, her favorite voice and words, those of Rabindranath Tagore, entered her mind: *You can't cross the sea merely by standing and staring at the water.*

The words resonated so strongly in Noor's mind that she almost choked on her rice. Tagore's voice vanished as suddenly as it had appeared. The void always left a hole in her heart. Sometimes it felt like Tagore's voice was the only thing keeping her alive.

Noor sighed and left the courtyard for the small room she shared with her roommate, Asha. It was right above the ashram's main entrance, on the first floor. Asha and Noor's room didn't contain very much, and it contained even less for Noor, whose "bed" comprised of sundry mismatched scraps of sheeting. Asha, on the other hand had an actual charpoy in the corner, covered by a net, a relative luxury, to save her from mosquitoes. Faded burnt-orange walls, the color of the Ganga sky at dawn, and bedsheets almost a century old, woven by local craftsmen from Varanasi, added the only stroke of character to the drab room. She had inherited all her belongings from the woman who had lived in the room before Noor. She had passed away, leaving her all her possessions, even the brass container Noor used to bring her Ganga water to the tulsi. She placed the holy book she carried with her everywhere on the floor beside her empty rice plate and her now empty brass water pot, and sat down on her sheets.

Presently, Noor heard footsteps and Asha entered the room and stood over her. Asha came from a wealthy family and this privilege was what infused her with an air of superiority.

Asha spoke at Noor from above, "Noor, everyone downstairs is talking about why you spent so much time at the ghat earlier today. Were you with a man? Are you seeing someone? You know that people will kill you if they find something sinful about you." Asha cackled at her own joke.

When Asha left the room, she heard her and the other women's shrill gossip as it echoed across the ashram's courtyard. But she didn't care. She just closed her ears, hoping to hear Tagore's soothing voice again, and, as she did, she lay down on her sheets to stare at the ceiling and thought of the word "tamasha."

The Temple of Fireflies

Sometimes visible, sometimes yours, sometimes equal

Anarkali was a subterranean inhabitant of the City of the Dead. She lived in an underground world beneath an underground street in an underground room without an address or electricity. Nor was it as if she required either; she never expected anyone to write her a mail to be delivered to her house, or to welcome any guests, or to give any vendor or solicitor any reason to descend the rickety bamboo ladder that lead to the deep, dark, dank place she called home.

The ceiling, if you could call it that, of Anarkali's home was an iron grate. Through it she could she see or hear the movements of the world above by studying the shifting shadows and the sounds they made.

Even after having lived in her underground dwelling for over thirty years, Anarkali had very few possessions. A couple of wood planks upon which she slept, the small rug she'd fastened to the main wall to soak up its dampness, and a modest stack of discarded sarees she had picked up from Lolark Kund—the deep, perfectly square, holy bath that lay at the bottom of a vertiginous labyrinth of steep steps, where women went to pray to beget sons. The women who went to Lolark Kund often left their old sarees on the steps. Many poor women and transgenders like herself would go in the night to pick up these. Anarkali had strung a plastic line across her room so she could hang and dry her chronically wet clothes, and had built a small shelf out of a rotting piece of wood to store her makeup.

Anarkali's favorite possession, out of the meager few she had, was an old, torn-and-faded ticket stub for a past screening of *Mughal-e-Azam*, India's majestic historical love story. She kept it tucked into the bronze frame of the small cracked mirror she used to prepare her face for her customers. Crouching in front of it, she would powder her face thickly with white talcum powder all the way up to her receding hairline, use black charcoal to draw in her missing eyebrows, rub pinkish rouge on her cheeks to hide her wrinkles and apply dark red lipstick to her lips. And then, if she remembered, she would pin fake flowers in her jet-black dyed hair. At least the ticket-stub tucked into the side of her mirror, along with the memories it carried, made her feel a little romantic, though her broken old mirror didn't always agree.

One day, through the grate above, Anarkali overheard a passerby claim that "a ghost lived down there." *Did they mean her?* Being thought of as a ghost didn't insult her. Not at all. It overjoyed her to hear it because it made her feel safe knowing that most people who passed over her home would neither risk their lives nor reputation by daring to enter Anarkali's subterranean habitat under the City of The Dead.

She loved her address-less, nameless room for many reasons, despite some in Varanasi fearing it. It made her invisible when she wanted to be, it sheltered her from predators (mostly of the human kind), it cooled her when summer burned others, and because it was conveniently located near the Sangam Chowk, the heart of the city, the crossroads between the new and old areas of town, it was free and clear of the main Ganga sewage system; though even that could sometimes suddenly change during the overflow season.

Some in Varanasi went so far as to call Anarkali's cherished home a "snake hole." Ironically, they were right—a black snake did visit her home sometimes. Sometimes she imagined the snake to be the most vicious king cobra and sometimes she thought that it was just a slithering illusion created by her imagination. Whatever kind of snake it was, Anarkali didn't even think to kill it, because, in her opinion, the snake's visits protected her, not harmed her. Anarkali viewed the snake as symbolic of the very beast Lord Shiva wore around his neck, as the embodiment of how important it was to face your fears. She had fears, yes, but not for snakes or other creatures that flew or slithered the earth. Her fear was reserved for humans.

While Anarkali saw the many benefits of living down below, there were also some detriments. She had to cover her bed with a roof of plastic sheets affixed to poles placed at each corner of her bed when it rained.

During the monsoon overflow season, sewage flowed in a stream on the floor right next to her bed, a flow she named "mini-Ganga." When Ganga *really* swelled over her banks, the flow would become so heavy that Anarkali had to flee before the whole room submerged in water. The temporary but absolute flooding of her home was the most challenging part of being a resident of the transgender *hijra* community. It was only during the most dangerous days of potential flood that she took her most precious possessions and moved in with the other hijras, or decided to sleep on the open terrace of Halwai Sweets, a confectionery on Sangam Chowk run by one of the fattest, most miserable and miserly residents of Varanasi, Ram Halwai. Anarkali was safe there, at least until Ram discovered she had been sleeping there.

Despite having to flee for her life on some occasions, Anarkali much preferred staying at her place, for its absolute gloominess always seemed to give way to the most unusual moments of magic. She enjoyed the continuous melodies created by the water dancing into her room, as well as the drops of water that clung to the grate before they finally fell to scatter the colorful reflections of the morning sun, as it stretched its beams down into her dark underground realm. Anarkali knew the sun had no desire to live with and warm her in her dungeon, but simply spread its light and visited its rays just to return some small unspoken favor. Somedays the sun's reluctant rays appeared like misty-winged angels, while on other days they appeared like small bent rainbows.

But it was during that most amazing part of summer, right before the monsoons began, when it was neither day nor night, during the birth and death of twilight, that the most magical thing occurred: Anarkali's dank little place would fill with fireflies, so many fireflies that her place became more like a firefly temple. And after her long work days amid summer's sweat and toil, and predators of the human sort, Anarkali would always anticipate returning home so she could simply relax on her wooden planks and stare and dream up into the natural starlit sky created by the flickering insect-magicians of light that for some reason had decided to make their home there. As far as she was concerned, like the snake, she would always welcome the fireflies and their soft fireworks show.

That particular day, Anarkali woke up early with the sunlight washing her room in more gold and pink than usual. She splashed her feet in the gutter of dirty water running past her home, and then positioned herself before her mirror to get ready for the day. Her young friend Choti would sometimes bring her makeup, wigs, and more rarely, luxuriously colored scarves she picked up at Manikarnika Ghat. Choti always seemed to consider her.

Anarkali pulled her hair back into a bun the way her mother always did, tied her torn-and-faded red saree around her waist, painted on a large vermilion bindi, lined her eyes with kohl, and smeared her lips red. She then took a small blue plastic container of white powder and used a stained cotton-puff to cake as much powder on her face as it could hold, becoming a flood of another kind. Anarkali, almost involuntarily, splashed so much powder on her sullen face that it not only hid her wrinkles, but also her shame, pain, and darkness, until her skin refused to accept more and the extra powder fell to earth like dead stardust.

Fully made up, Anarkali climbed up the bamboo ladder to a world not waiting for her. She pushed aside the grate, the manhole lid she called her front door, and climbed up and out, reborn on the streets above. Her eyes squinted at the bright sun's glare as she shoved the grate back in place and sealed it shut.

Shaking out the folds of her saree and then pulling the free end of her *pallu*, the edge of her saree, tighter around her chest, she walked briskly out into the pathos of daily life: heading toward Sangam Chowk, where she often panhandled with Choti.

Sangam Chowk was always bustling with local traders and business people due to its close proximity to Varanasi's main bus station. Sangam was Anarkali's "turf," and contained the last traffic signal before the ghats, as well as the first signal back toward the city, depending on which direction you were headed.

Anarkali walked with a slight limp, favoring one side and keeping her gait as stable as possible for a person walking briskly to a job she detested. This was due to an injury she'd received at the merciless end of a hard stick. As she neared her Chowk, Raja, the head local cop, in his crisp khaki police uniform, was already stalking her from astride his motorcycle. As he passed, Raja wielded his stick and hit Anarkali across her bad arm and sped away.

"Can't you see my hand and arm have already been broken? You hit me right there! What did your mother eat before giving birth to you, you shameless bastard!" Anarkali yelled as Raja plunged into the traffic.

Raja swiveled his head around, "It's what *your* mother *forgot* to eat! Let me know where you want me to hit you next time, because I always will whenever and wherever I please," Raja yelled back, grinning lasciviously and smoothing his mustache. Further ahead at a cigarette kiosk, Raja stopped his motorbike. The skinny vendor handed him a pack of Wills cigarettes and a *paan*—the red-saliva-generating plug of tobacco and areca nut wrapped in a betel leaf that its users packed in their mouths between their cheek and gums; as much a part of culture as Amitabh Bachchan was, and actually had a song dedicated to it, this product that kept many people spitting its juices on walls and streets everywhere in India. It was Raja's favorite song, one he would often sing as he chewed his paan, "*Khaai kaay paan Banaras walaaa*," which roughly translated to "After eating a Varanasi paan…"

"Everything okay?" Raja said to the paan-vendor, chewing his paan with great relish.

"All because of your blessings, Sahibji," said the vendor.

Raja gunned his throttle and sped off toward the police station without paying. Between hitting Anarkali and stiffing vendors, Raja filled his days with his favorite daily rituals of harassing the public and demanding his commission for "permitting" people to do their jobs on his turf. Every day after Raja left, the vendors looked straight at Anarkali in sympathetic understanding.

Soon after Anarkali started to work Sangam Chowk, she developed a hard-won, but now thoroughly tested and very efficient strategy that allowed her to know when a customer would part with money, based on the direction and flow of traffic, and an assessment of whether people stopped on one side of the signal or the other.

Further, in her general begging assessments, Anarkali had started to determine and categorize her "begees." There were the Departers, those headed to the ghats for funerals and cremation—be careful begging from them, she cautioned, they were shattered. The loss of their loved ones or the awaited death of their benefactor made them edgy and indecisive, and at their worst, violent. It had proven prudent to wait for them as they headed back from the ghats, that is only if the cremation priest hadn't already emptied their pockets. To convert these Departers into Temporary Givers it was a good idea to say, *"Bhagwan unki aatma ko shanti de,"* may God rest their soul in peace.

After begging for so many years, Anarkali could easily tell, to her benefit and safety, who was on their way back from a cremation, or the ritualistic spreading of a loved one's ashes over the Ganga. Caught just after that moment, these Temporary Givers, whether due to their fleeting realization of life's arbitrariness, or their sense of loss, grief, or guilt, were the best givers and the most susceptible to having their money begged out of them. The

Temporary Givers almost always gave something. But if these same givers encountered Anarkali a day or two *after* they had returned from the banks, and had returned to their dissolved mirages of vast inherited wealth or material, they immediately saw through her insincerity, and not one rupee came forth.

Anarkali had to strike when the iron of loss was at its hottest.

Welcomers, as Anarkali had branded them with a beaming grin, though they had not proven themselves the most generous, were certainly the most pleasant "begees" at Sangam Chowk. Welcomers were typically mothers taking their newborn babies to the ghats seeking Ganga's blessings. They considered it auspicious to sight a hijra, and Anarkali certainly was one. Anytime she caught sight of a baby in the arms of its mother, she presented herself clamorously in that direction, doing whatever it took to get their attention—singing, dancing, beating a drum, or ringing a bell. Anarkali loved babies anyhow, rupees or no rupees.

Then there were the tourists wandering aimlessly around, killing time. Anarkali dubbed these more passive wanderers, Time Passers, or TPs, for short. (Sometimes the monikers she created stuck, sometimes they didn't.) There was nothing particularly challenging or unchallenging about begging from TPs, but what seemed to be true was that the poorer they were, the more likely they were to be on foot, and thus pass closer by Anarkali, whereas the richer TPs had the benefit of distancing themselves from the din and dust of the outside world—especially the strange noise of flamboyant begging hijras—behind the glass windows of their cars.

Finally, Anarkali had classified the Privileged Ones—the many Westerners who visited India on a "spiritual" journey, and who afterwards felt greatly relieved to finally get back home, to live out their newly cleansed, sedate, and predictable lives. Puzzlingly, if they were fresh off the boat Privileged Ones, they were either very generous, or not generous at all. Anarkali had figured out that this depended on whether Varanasi was their first stop in India; or if they had already exhausted their bodies, souls, and monies learning yoga and meditation, and visiting the famous Golden Triangle of Jaipur, Agra, and New Delhi.

"See how people live in poverty here and you are still so thankless!" Anarkali sometimes chided the more ungenerous of the Privileged Ones.

For some reason though, if and when Anarkali ever decided to grant them a picture alongside her, they always paid, and Anarkali never understood why.

Anarkali had taken up her usual position at the intersection by the traffic lights when she saw Choti hurtling toward her; she was obviously in a bad mood because she was banging on every window of every car she passed.

The two had become good friends the moment they had first encountered each other on the rough, smoky streets of Varanasi. And after they'd learned to trust each other, Anarkali had shared all the tricks of her trade, everything she knew about the craft of begging, all her strategies, her customer categories, and nicknames with Choti—and to

Anarkali's surprise, the diminutive tight-rope-walker had mastered them all.

Anarkali spied a hippy, a white guy lounging in the back of a stalled rickshaw with his arms and legs hanging loosely and his head flung black. Most of these types had long beards, long hair, and wore colorful scarves and shorts. There were many such hippies living or passing through Varanasi all the time, and Anarkali immediately approached him and struck a pose, one that was typically inspired by any of a number of currently trending Bollywood actresses: left hand on hip, and right finger suggestively under her pouted lips, "Hey young man!" Anarkali said. "You are one creamy hot vanilla ice cream. You are so hot you are melting."

The young man groaned.

"Anyway, sweetheart, may you get a perfect wife someday. Today is Saturday, so for two rupees, I will bless you for it to happen faster. Two rupees is a cheap deal to get you the perfect wife. My arm is broken, or otherwise I would have danced for you as well. How about it? Two rupees to meet the perfect wife?"

The signal turned green and the rickshaw carrying the limp unresponsive body of the young man accelerated through the intersection, almost grazing Anarkali, who still held out for at least one rupee from him.

A dejected Anarkali walked up to Choti, who was still venting her frustration on the lineup of car windows, even though the cars had started to move forward. "Choti, you're back," Anarkali said. "What happened with the tight-rope walking?" Anarkali began counting the money she had collected so far, right under Choti's nose.

"I'm never going to work with that bloody thief Chintu, anymore. He took my share of the money and escaped on a boat in the Ganga, I have a strong feeling he is going to gamble away all our money and get in trouble with the police," Choti vented her frustration.

"I've told you so many times, one day you will fall off that rope, and when you fall back to earth there will be no one to take care of you and you will end up just like Guddu over there," Anarkali replied.

Choti looked at Guddu, the old cripple who sat on a single wooden plank with a mismatched set of wheels attached underneath, in the middle of the cow-hoof beaten footpath that led into one side of Anarkali's turf. Guddu was completely paralyzed due to a spine injury and had to be wheeled around by others everywhere he went. Today, strangely, he was all alone.

"Anarkali, I'll never fall as far down as Guddu, I'm a bird, remember?" Choti's humor found her again, and now she laughed, spread and flapped her arms, pretended to fly away, and began to dance.

Anarkali laughed, opening her mouth wide and throwing her head back, then beckoned Choti through the open rickshaw she had convinced to stop. "Choti, stop flying like a bird and come back to earth. It's time to go to work." The light had turned red, which meant that the traffic would stop and they could implement their begging strategy.

Choti ran back to take up a position on the traffic's farthest flank, and the two started to work the traffic from both sides, knocking on every car window, shouting into every rickshaw or at people riding on the back of motor-

THE TEMPLE OF FIREFLIES

taxis—generally harassing anyone who crossed their path for rupees, no matter their category or status.

"From now on, Choti, this is not *my* territory, it is our territory," Anarkali said.

Choti grinned.

"It's just unfortunate we have to pay Inspector Raja 50% of everything we make, but that's my extortion agreement with him," said Anarkali, as she relentlessly propositioned each of her targeted customers with a raucous high-pitched, flirtatious laugh.

"Raja is the worst man, he should be called 'Ravana,'" Choti growled, referring to the ten-headed demon from the epic, *Ramayana*. Choti continued, "We burn our flesh under the sun for a few rupees and he gets half of it—I have half-a-mind not to give that Ravana any of my share next time around. I've had it up to here with him and the Chintus of the world. Maybe Raja is that bastard Chintu's secret father."

"I wouldn't doubt it," said Anarkali.

"And he keeps threatening to lock me up for the rude replies I give him when he and his boys come to break up my tamasha. He'll be lucky if I don't break up his tamasha one day. He can't arrest me for opening my own mouth, can he?" Choti said.

"I'm sure a bastard like Raja or one of his bastard, potbellied boys could find a way," Anarkali said.

"The sun and smoke from the pyres must have driven him crazy. He used to be more reasonable. The pumpkin he married must have turned his brain into a pumpkin as well," Choti said with a loud laugh.

"Choti! Hush your mouth!" Anarkali said. "You'll get into so much trouble for talking so brazenly all the time. Listen, if you go to the other side of the street you can make more money. Those people over there are TPs arriving from cremations."

"How do you know?"

"I can smell them. They are ripe for begging. I'll stay on this side, deal?" Anarkali said.

"No no no, I can't go to that side. Ram Sweets is on that side, and I already had a fight with him over the sweet *jalebi* I tried to steal. You know Indian funnel cakes are my weakness," Choti said.

"Then why aren't you fat?" Anarkali said.

Choti shrugged. "Ram Halwai even hit me. Cheapster! He makes twenty jalebis at a time, what difference does losing one make? I know he keeps all his money in that big red box he holds close to his big fat stomach, and he'll be lucky if I don't punch him in the gut and steal all his rupees one day. What comes around, goes around. He hit me even on the day his father died, and he had already been giving away all away his sweets for free, anyway."

Anarkali slapped her hands across her ears and winced. "Choti, do you ever stop? You're going to drive all of Varanasi crazy and bring all of Varanasi's dead back to life with all these schemes you can't stop spouting off about. Halwai is a rich man, you should respect him."

"The only thing I respect about Ram Halwai is his big fat hairy stomach, it's like an old, moss-covered earthen pot with a tap."

"His gut is a tap?" Anarkali shook her head, utterly confused.

"Not his gut, the button that sticks out of it," Choti said, laughing and flicking up her right-hand pinky.

Anarkali screwed up her face, caught her tongue between her front teeth and hissed with laughter. "Oh, *that* kind of tap. *Eeww!* You're so bad. I would never drink from Halwai's dirty tap."

"Me, neither, but I would consider stealing some of his sweet money out from under it for what he did to me."

Anarkali reached into the neck of the short-cropped blouse that she wore with her saree, and took out two rupees. "Choti, go buy yourself some samosas for lunch. You must be hungry and that is why you are so cranky at the world today," she said.

Choti took the rupees and tucked them in her belt, "I don't like to accept favors from anyone, but Anarkali, you are like my family. I'll return the money to you when I get my share from Chintu—and after I kill him," she said.

Anarkali smiled, and turned back to continue her aggressive begging. She didn't reveal it very often, but the truth was that she had more love in her heart for Choti than for anyone, even more than she had for her hijra sisters.

Choti ran across the street to the chai-wallah. On the way back with the hot treats wrapped in a newspaper, Choti stopped at a traditional old spice shop that displayed colorful mounds of spices.

Before the owner noticed, Choti slyly scooped a small handful of bright yellow turmeric powder from its mound and slipped away, checking the street for the break in traffic that would allow her safest passage back to Anarkali.

On the other side of the street, Choti saw a mother and her toddler daughter also waiting to cross, the toddler whining and refusing to hold her mother's hand. When the break in traffic came, the mother grabbed her daughter's hand and led her across the road, passing by Choti as she crossed from the opposite side. As they passed one another, Choti couldn't help but admire how tightly the mother held her daughter's hand in order to protect and guide her. Choti had never felt such a hand on hers, so she was fascinated by the way people's hands interlocked, and paid very close attention to it. This fascination always ended with Choti reaching over and clasping her own hands together, for she had no outside hands to hold, or other hands to hold hers. Was this a sad thing? She didn't think about it.

Finally, Choti ran back across the intersection to find Anarkali taking a break, resting against a crooked pole, dead tired and staring blankly at the ground.

Choti held out the turmeric in the calloused palms of her hands. "Anarkali," she said.

"Hmm?" Anarkali looked up.

"I got something special for you."

"Turmeric?" said Anarkali.

"It will help your arm and hand."

"That's very kind of you," Anarkali said, squeezing her tired eyes shut as if to fight back tears, suddenly overcome. "Did you have a samosa?"

Choti laughed, "Yes, and I didn't even have to spend one rupee."

Anarkali grinned and raised an eyebrow. "Really?"

"I put on my 'poor-sad-and-hungry' face to a Welcomer, and they gave me samosas to fulfill their dead father's wishes! I drooped my mouth and made my face even poorer, sadder, and hungrier so they would give me an extra samosa for you. Works every time!" Choti returned all the money, plus turmeric and a delicious samosa into Anarkali's hands.

Anarkali munched off a corner of the samosa Choti had given her and started to apply the turmeric to her wounded arm. "Choti, my girl, my best friend, you are right. Everyone becomes more generous the moment they lose someone."

"Hmm," Choti said, nodding with her mouth full.

"Did you feed any of your samosa crumbs to your pets?" Anarkali said, still rubbing turmeric on her hand and arm, which were turning yellow. What would another daub of color on her body matter?

"My pets?" Choti said, bouncing on her toes, confused.

"The lice you keep in your hair," Anarkali spluttered with laughter.

Choti laughed, too. "Anarkali, I don't understand why these rich people always wait for their father to die before offering food to others who are hungry. Why does showing a generous spirit always have to be related to a loss?"

"Because of religion, my *laddoo*, my sweet. Religion is the most misguiding compass," Anarkali said. "We can get away with everything in the name of religion; even murder. Just wash away your sins in the Ganga then go back and commit more sins."

"Seems too easy," Choti said.

"You're right. They all come here to wash their sins in the holy Ganga," Anarkali said. "I take part in it, too. I misguide people with the same compass, for my own benefit. My tamasha is using the same idea to scare and curse and coax rupees out of people. Given my situation, our situation, is it a sin? Who cares!"

Suddenly, without warning, Anarkali spun around, almost flinging what was left of her turmeric like Holi powder, in order to pounce on some new passersby—a middle-aged couple who were obvious devotees. "God will give you so much more! A son! A car! Your own bungalow!"

Anarkali's repeated shrieks shrank them back in their tracks, and the man tightened his grip on his wife and fled away.

Anarkali laughed. "See the violence some see in my blessings? You'd think everyone wants the same things in life. Choti, what do you want?"

"All I want in life is for my lice to die, I am tired of scratching my head," Choti said. "By the way, after Ram Halwai saw me running back with the rupees I didn't have to spend, he got so worried that his belly shook, and as soon as he saw me, he held his red money box even closer to his tap."

Anarkali and Choti had a great laugh.

The Birth of Light

*Everything is born out of darkness,
even the light*

It was near day's end in Varanasi and time for the *aarti* ritual to begin. Its ringed formations and offerings and blessings of reverent fire, flickering lamps, candlelight, flame, and song, would create a starry-eyed parade of ritual worship, individual and collective, that would send floating and lifting the soft glow of diya candles great and small throughout the ghats and all the way to Ganga's edge. The onset of aarti even frightened away the sun, who was finally relieved of its daytime duties, and the last flocks of birds, whom the sun's dying pink rays had illuminated into shadow, flew away home to their nests.

During aarti, every vendor's stall switched to offer only trays containing the delightful, glowing, ghee-dipped, cotton-wick earthen lamps that cast the small grouping of flowers at their centers in hypnotic swaying light. Taken together, it was these glowing trays of many small diyas being passed in reverent circular motion that set the aarti's resplendence aglow. Musicians and priests polished their prayer instruments, soft-drink vendors packed their bottle crates with ice, and the young boys who were training to become priests set the pedestals for the pandits—all were set for the evening aarti.

When it finally began, the ghats transformed into floating shoals and moving constellations of light, chant, reflection, closure, hope, and forgiveness, as every ghat at Ma Ganga's edge filled with flames, flowers, and light's devotion, like stars come to earth.

The twilight also rang the starting bell for the hordes of worshipful and not so worshipful tourists and residents that aarti at Varanasi's eighty-odd ghats beckoned. The ghats would be overrun, and Choti, Anarkali, and others from their world, would take full advantage.

The cremations of Manikarnika continued, unaffected by the ceremonies happening everywhere, adding their own dark smoke and flame to the more charming aarti smoke and flames.

As the aarti played out, so too did the conflict between Anarkali and Inspector Raja at Sangam Chowk.

Raja sat at his desk in the police station he commanded. Behind him on the wall, among some random portraits of officers adorned with dried flower and glittering paper garlands, hung an oversized photograph of Raja's father, Shiv, a legendary Varanasi police officer who, like Raja, had created his own laws for his own enrichment and convenience. Also like Raja, Shiv would often arrive home drunk, without any consideration for his waiting family. Shiv loved to tell his family as well as everyone else that he would one day become the "King of Varanasi," and if he ever had a son, that son, in all ways, would be the Prince to his King. This is not to say that Shiv was being patriotic and expressing himself out of chivalry for the good of the nation. To him, and eventually his son, chivalry was defined not by courage to protect the weak, but by the ability to extract the last drop of the weak one's blood, using both fear and the law.

Raja had learned his policing from watching his paternal hero speak and wield his police power among his enemies and friends, and of course the local citizens, whom he referred to as his "subjects," and whom he would beat down and kick like dogs, abusing children and elders alike. Before embarking on any new exploitation, Raja always glanced back at the photograph of his father for inspiration and approval.

Raja called for tea and went through his files. The one atop his pile pertained to some men who had been racing around, siren blaring, with a fake government security light affixed to the roof of their car. Three out-of-towners had been arrested for the crime, and Raja asked his constable, *"Ameer ghar kay ladkay hain, kya?"* (Are they the sons of the rich?)—to which the fidgeting constable replied, "Yes, yes, Inspector Raja, they are just a bunch of young kids from decent homes who were having fun and made a foolish mistake."

Everyone laughed when Raja signed the file with his orders to set them free.

Raja signaled to his constable. "Get your partner, it's time to go out and collect the weekly fines. We'll hit Sangam Chowk first," Raja said in a low voice, and his constable nodded.

It was the holiest of holy days—the best, most lucrative day for the police to shake down very beggar, sadhu, street vendor, tour guide, really anyone who was alive, and whom Raja's forces could get their hands on to collect their weekly "fines." All were guilty of something, and the fines served as commissions to the police that bought the citizens freedom to see another day. After his father had died, Prince Raja had become the new king, and no one dared ask him about what his fines were for, and so far, the Prince and his minions had never failed to collect.

Raja was a true force of penetrating evil—the heartless-blessing his mother's many visits and offerings to Lolark Kund had produced. Like many other women hoping to beget a son, Raja's mother, Nandini, had ascended and descended the steps of Lolark Kund for ten years, praying for a male child before she gave birth to him; all so that her son might one day continue the Pandeys' proud family tradition.

Inspector Raja sped along on his motorbike flanked by two junior officers in triangular formation. They saw Anarkali and slowed to a stop behind her. "Anarkali, there are too many complaints piling up against you. You are becoming a menace to society."

Anarkali had been forcing her usual blessings on a couple bound for the evening aarti in the back of the rickshaw; an overture that had not pleased the rickshaw-puller or the couple, and now they were all engaged in a heated argument. When they escaped Anarkali's still-rupee-less grasp, Anarkali turned around to glare at Raja and his boys. "You scared them away!"

Raja sneered at her, and he and his boys shook their heads.

"You know who the real menaces to society are?" Anarkali said. "You and your goons, your brainless *chamchas*!"

Inspector Raja became angry enough to dismount his bike. "I'm no snake-charmer, but your tongue is becoming as venomous as a cobra's," Raja said. "And I'd be happy to cut it out for you." The inspector crossed his arms, laughed and looked at his boys, who laughed and folded their arms on cue. The bigger of Raja's chamchas interrupted: "We know where you live," he said, and the three chamchas continued to trade condescending glances, smirks as sharp as knives cutting across their mouths.

Raja's words made Anarkali nervous, and she started to quiver inside her saree. It didn't help that she had only eaten a corner of a samosa that day.

"Look, just leave me alone," Anarkali said. "You always create unnecessary trouble for all of us who have to scrounge the streets or walk the air for our livelihood, and it's you in particular who brings out the worst in me. Just seeing your face or hearing the buzz of your motorbike makes me absolutely surly."

Raja lifted his chin and narrowed his eyes, leering at the eunuch.

"And you hit me so hard yesterday that my arm can barely move anymore. How can I survive with one arm? Just tell me who I can report you to, and I would be pleased to do so. *Anything* so you will bloody just leave me alone," Anarkali said.

Raja folded his arms across his chest and laughed with all his arrogance, wielding his stick. At the sight of it, Anarkali flinched and winced.

"Did you forget my name?" Raja said. "My name is Raja and I am the king around here. You haven't paid my men going on four weeks now. If I don't get what you owe me by tomorrow, you can no longer beg in this chowk, you hear? Like my officer said, 'We know where you live,' secretly and illegally."

Anarkali straightened herself. "Really? And does your pumpkin wife know the secret of what you do? At night? Besides illegally extorting and beating all of who have to survive out here? You're not even a complete man, you know…" Anarkali said.

At once Raja told his goons to leave and then said, stroking his mustache, and leaning into Anarkali: "Listen, you whore, I'll be waiting for you behind the gym later, as soon as the aarti ends and the security guards leave the ghats. You'd better be there. My advice for between now and then is to shut your mouth and stop talking like some kind of snake. Hear me?"

Anarkali nodded, just barely.

"That's a good girl," said Inspector Raja, and he revved his bike and sped away with his goons in tow to hassle any other beggar they came across.

Anarkali muttered to herself: "I wish the myth that a simple curse could destroy a dynasty were true. I curse you, Raja, and those you serve, every minute I am alive."

THE BIRTH OF LIGHT

Anarkali limped under the nearby bypass holding her bad arm and sat down on the curb. She opened out her cloth bag and fingered the turmeric powder and what remained of the extra samosa that Choti, in all her gruff sweetness, had forced her to take.

Anarkali continued muttering to herself, this time reciting a little poem:

While the immortal gods camouflage themselves in temples,
And mortal humans in their homes,
It's the atheist creatures on the streets
who need the strongest belief...

The aarti had was in full swing across the ghats. The crowd chanted and lit their lamps and fires, and soon the throngs of people on the banks of the Ganga ebbed and flowed like a land-bound sea. Hundreds of traditional, brightly-colored wooden rowing boats led by the tour guides, set their anchors on the far banks for the best views.

Now it was time for the other children from the Nameless House with Pink Walls, who Choti still had to reckon with on the streets sometimes, and who often dressed up as Shiva, Parvati, Hanuman, Krishna, or Lakshmi—the major deities of the Hindu pantheon—to fan out and beg from tourists and devotees alike. Choti believed the guises her former peers wore earned them more rupees not because the donors necessarily held any positive belief in that certain god or goddess, but out of the fear that if they didn't pay up, they would be branded with a curse. They paid out of fear, not reverence.

The god-orphans had themselves stitched the vibrant clothes they wore to match their masks, from the fabric that the relatives of the deceased had pinned and knotted or wrapped their loved ones in for their final journey to Manikarnika Ghat. It was also quite easy to find fake hair pieces, ornaments, and crowns the dead had been dressed in here and the orphans used these to embellish their Hindu god costumes. The ornamentation her peers preferred did make the begging life more dream-like—both for the beggar and "begee"—but now that Chintu had disappeared from her life, Choti believed more firmly in Anarkali's opinion that, "...dressing up in the clothes and masks of gods takes too much energy, and allows the lines that form across the sweating human faces underneath to expose the real masks, so all the effort goes to waste."

Whether Anarkali was right or wrong, even without a mask, Choti was exhausted. She begged near the tourist buses, which she knew would spit up tourists headed for the ghats and Ganga to witness the thousands of flickering golden flames of aarti. She saw a seemingly blissful, beautiful family walk by; the kind of family where the grandparents try to hold the hands of every family member, as if affectionately attempting to impart the depth and richness of their family culture to them just by touching hands.

During aarti, the spirituality and peace-seeking visitors, especially families like the one she had been admiring, would many times offer her their children's unfinished chips or food or half-drunk bottles of soda, so, naturally, Choti approached, because she was always hungry.

THE BIRTH OF LIGHT

What upset the young tight-rope-walker was that sometimes, before she could reach her hand out or utter one word or flash one pathetic face to this family—before her shadow had barely approached—the mother would draw back her kids: "Don't, you'll catch a disease!" Once, when this happened, one of the children, about Choti's size and age, turned back to look at her, and for a second she and the child held each other's eyes. Choti assumed this to be a "moment of understanding," but how could that possibly be true and how could she ever know?

Then, just as soon as the cycle of giving and forgiving and everything associated with aarti had commenced, it dwindled to its end, at least for that day, leaving another cycle to commence, as the chaos and bustle of traffic again overwhelmed the daily dose of spirituality, patience, and tolerance, which had rapidly faded away after everyone dowsed their flames and left the ghats.

Choti had left the Nameless House two weeks after Chintu's disappearance. She had waited for him, her anger turning to worry, but there was still no sign of him. When she lay down to sleep at night, Chintu's empty bed made her think of the most horrible things. She knew in the back of her mind that Chintu was in trouble with the police but she didn't want to acknowledge it. She would deliberately imagine herself walking her tight-rope, feeling lighter and lighter... till she could close her eyes and her tiny body went to sleep. Finally, one day, she had felt his absence so acutely that she decided not to stay there anymore. The usual irritants too were more unbearable without him.

What she had hated most was that the Nameless Man always had the children form a line-up so the Privileged Ones, the guilty-eyed visiting Westerners, could stand amid all of them, smiling while having their photographs taken with the orphans.

It was all so pretentious.

One time, when Chintu had been around, the children had been feasting on some fried breads and chickpea curry they had collected from the devotees at the ghats when suddenly the Nameless Man shouted down at them from the attic, "After your morning Ganga bath, you all have to come back to meet the social workers!"

Chintu had groaned aloud. He had especially disliked this photo-op with the social workers—the visits could also be from Western tourists, devotees, or locals—because he resented the surface lies, fake promises, and feel-good commitments that were always made but never led to anything. They'd arrive bearing their genuine smiles but false promises to see these kids in their tattered clothes, their voices echoing through the courtyard as they cautiously tiptoed around the angry cow to greet the assembled children.

"You are so pretty and nice," one might say. "So, so sweet, can we adopt you?"

"Mama, we should take them home with us," the child of another visitor would say.

"I will come back here every day. Will you be my friend?"

No, Choti would think.

"I will bring you a cake on your birthday, what flavor do you like?"

THE BIRTH OF LIGHT

These types of comments, which always lasted until the last photo was taken, always made Chintu cringe. These instant friendships and put-on sympathies never lasted beyond the photo-op, he told Choti his face red with anger. It was all a show—no one would come back, no promises were kept, no cakes were delivered, and no saving adoptions transpired. Though she and Chintu didn't believe them one bit, the smaller kids were genuinely hurt when the visitors never kept their promises.

Even at that age, Choti had sensed that what the visitors really wanted was to ease their own guilt, a guilt that was somehow alleviated by being surrounded by poor, invisible children. To Choti that idea was just plain weird.

A few days after Chintu's disappearance, Choti had been herded in with the rest of the children to get their picture taken. "I won't be having my picture taken, I *hate* it! I *hate* standing there like a sad and lifeless pathetic prop without a voice or a heart. I want to fly!" she shouted.

The Nameless Man replied, "Choti, how do you think we pay for letting you stay at The Nameless House with Pink Walls? If you won't line up for a photo with the rest of the children, then you might as well leave."

All the Nameless Man's sharp words did was convince Choti she was not coming back the next morning. That same day, when Choti returned from her frantic begging with Anarkali to the Nameless House with Pink Walls, she lay on her aching back with her tired legs and sore feet stretched out, and said to herself, "All I want to do is walk on my rope, like birds fly in the air, free and fearless."

That was Choti's last day at The Nameless House with Pink Walls.

That evening, a dejected Choti climbed up a tree into her "sky nest," the new little aerial dwelling she had built in a sprawling Banyan across from the ghats, a veritable nest made of rags, cardboard and a sheet of plastic, and littered with the discarded possessions of the deceased she had scavenged from Manikarnika Ghat. She had built her dwelling in a tree—no one in Varanasi could climb a tree as fast as Choti, she was a tight-rope-walker after all. The tree she had chosen overlooked the open-air, police gym and wrestling pit that spread out across a courtyard behind the police station.

In the beginning, Choti had hoped to be able to practice her tight-rope-walking in the limbs of the tree, but beneath its traditional veneer, this cop's gym was no ordinary *akhara*—it was the wrestling pit where all of Raja's cops who "served" the ghats competed with one another to become the ultimate physical specimens of mankind, potbellies notwithstanding.

Now safely in her sky-nest, Choti looked around the innards of the massive tree that sheltered her, its leafy branches seeming to multiply and spread out forever, and through that forever, she watched the ever-changing moon. *What could be better than one forever multiplied by another forever?* Choti thought.

Somedays she was haunted by the dead, other days she was haunted by the living, and still other days she just dwelled with no particular feeling, above the backyard gym of the police station in a tree where bats often woke her in the morning with their high-pitched squeals that only a few creatures can even hear. Fortunately, or unfortunately, Choti was one such creature and she had to admit, she too had become very much like a bat—fortunately because, being a night-dweller, she could welcome the rising sun and witness how the always dancing waters of Ganga showered the dawn sky with the colors reflecting across her surface; and unfortunately, because she always got less sleep than anyone else she knew.

As she toiled during the day, knocking on car windows for money, Choti always wondered why the world seemed to be going blind to those who deserved the widest-open eyes.

In all her tamashas, high or low, Choti had been no reclusive nocturnal bird, she was as highly visible as a peacock or a Bollywood celebrity, but at the same time she didn't exist at all. When night fell, the truth of things seemed to appear, especially the truth of her invisibility. And that's the way she preferred it. At night, all Choti wished for was to be invisible, mostly because she feared Ganga's dark side.

What Choti identified most with, and probably why she named her tiny dwelling the "sky-nest," were the caged songbirds she would, when she had earned enough rupees, occasionally buy just so she could set them free. She wanted to witness them once again flutter their wings and spread their songs into the world. But she wasn't naïve. Not at all. Because afterwards she would sell the empty cages back to the vendors to get part of her investment in the birds' liberation back. In Choti's diminutive chest, beat the heart of a freedom fighter. All she dreamed of was to be just like the free, singing bird, though she had already learned the hard way that such freedom came with the constant threat of predators.

The biggest challenge to Choti's sky-nest peace was the early-morning potbellied-police-officers' exercise regimen. She found it ridiculous, their shouting and chest-puffing as they ribbed each other, attempting to display their power and camaraderie. The cops' traditional manner of dress, Choti found even more ridiculous, so ridiculous she had once nearly fallen off her perch thinking about it. The cops wrapped their potbellies with a long strip of red cloth, which they first wrapped around their genitals then around their hips like a diaper. And they wore nothing else!

Choti couldn't help staring at the sight of the sweating, almost naked, exercising cops as they rolled around the clay-and-sand surface, wrestling and grunting, as they hoisted their weights of concrete and wood, or generally showed-off by flexing their muscles—that made their potbellies stick out even more—but it was always through the gaps of the fingers she had spread across her face out of shame. The potbellied police herd would sometimes corral themselves into their gym as early as 4:30 am. They were truly annoying, but the obnoxious grunts they emitted along with their taut breaths in and taut breathes out had become Choti's alarm clock, and she had learned to wake up silently enough to avoid detection.

THE BIRTH OF LIGHT

Choti didn't collect many things. Why would she? She never knew when she might suddenly be made to leave. One thing she did keep, her prized possession, was her battered, one-eyed teddy bear. Before she had met Anarkali, her dirty teddy, even with one eye missing and cotton wool stuffing oozing out of the ripped seams, had become her best friend, like the sibling she never had, like Chintu who had vanished from her life. She had found it while sorting through the garbage outside Manikarnika.

One night she had rolled over in her sleep, pushed by a dream, and dropped her teddy into the gym yard. When she woke the next day, she saw that the cops were tearing it apart and yelping like a pack of hungry guard dogs.

This, Choti could not let go so easily.

Later that day, while begging on the Chowk, she stole some red chilli powder from a spice vendor. When she returned to the gym after the cops had left for the day, she snuck across the gym and rubbed the burning powder all over their red-ribbon-thongs. She was so excited about her sweet-spicy revenge the next morning that she couldn't sleep. Choti knew the churlish cops would only blame it on one another. It was probably something one of them, if they were ever clever enough to, would have done to the rest of his cohorts sometime anyway.

The next morning, soon after her grunting alarm clock went off, Choti delighted in watching the huge potbellied men half-dressed and clutching themselves in their streaming, burning-hot red diapers, racing toward the Ganga to cool off their genitals. The scene was almost worth losing her teddy over, but Choti released not one laugh. She couldn't afford the risk.

More disturbing than the irritating sound of the cops' early morning routine was the sound of Raja and his chamchas voices mingling with Anarkali's voice, rising up to wake her in the middle of the night! At that deep hour, cradled in the limbs of her sky-nest, Choti was usually too tired to know what was going on—and this time, she was too frightened to even want to know.

Choti never asked Anarkali why she met those villains in the night, and she never revealed to Anarkali that she knew that Anarkali did. It took all of her restraint not to jump down to Anarkali's aid that night, when she witnessed Raja tugging at Anarkali's saree as she tried to fend him off while he verbally abused her in a drunken, deeply offensive way. "Run, where you will! Get out of here, bitch! We'll see how far you go!" Choti had heard Raja say.

The repeating episode tore at Choti's heart all the time, and she could only imagine how it tore at Anarkali's. But Choti remained mute on the terrible episodes in front of her best friend because it disturbed her too much to think about it, and, as far as Anarkali knew, she still lived in The Nameless House with Pink Walls. Choti didn't dare share the location of her secret hideaway with anyone. If Raja ever found out he would beat her mercilessly, or worse.

Anarkali was not easy to hang out with anymore. She looked tired and haunted. Choti was scared for her friend but didn't know what to do. Many a times Anarkali would not even show up for work.

Nor could Choti walk her tight-rope or win rupees from her tamasha crowds for a while because she had to find a new partner, hopefully one who wasn't a bloody thief. *But before I find a new tamasha partner, I am going to get all of my money back from Chintu. That's that. Period. And then I might kill him*, she thought.

So Choti found herself thinking about spending time with her new friend, the kind and gentle Noor, and one morning, a few days later she set out to do just that. As the policemen below made their early morning grunting animal sounds in their red ribbons and began to show off their strength to one another, Choti quietly descended from her nest and headed toward Manikarnika Ghat.

Choti reached the ghat and descended the stairs through the smoke, the parading corpses, and hawking vendors to sit in her usual spot by the Ganga. Sure enough, Noor appeared a few meters down the riverbank in her white saree, with her shaved head and her recently filled water pot. The old widow smiled as soon as she saw Choti's face, and her smile grew broader as she neared her on the steps.

"Choti, my girl, did you drown your Chintu yet?" Noor said, with a half smile.

Choti opened her mouth and laughed. "No Madamji, not yet. But you know I want to!"

Noor held a small newspaper-wrapped parcel in her hand. "I have something for you," she said.

"Yes, Madamji, what is it?" Choti said.

Noor handed the parcel to Choti.

Noor's kindness turned Choti into the excited fervor-filled child she might have been in another life, and her lips and hands trembled as she started to open the gift, too touched to speak, and steeling her eyes to any tears that wanted to pour out of them. From out of the plain wrapper bloomed a pair of blue rubber slippers.

"Thank you, these are so nice," Choti said. "The bottoms will make perfect weapons to hit Chintu with when I find him, bloody thief. Besides that, they are my favorite shade of blue."

Noor looked away and nodded. "That, I wouldn't know anything about. But it's better to wear them and not waste the comfort they might provide across Chintu's face. Wear them for yourself. I hope they are your size, I had to guess," Noor said.

Choti worked the slippers onto her calloused feet and gave Noor the thumbs-up sign. "They're a perfect fit," she said.

The sight of Choti's grimy little thumb shooting into the air brought a smile to Noor's face. "Good. I picked right, I guess." Choti inverted her new blue slippers to admire their soles, mesmerized by the sight and feel of the brand new blue rubber.

"Girl, what is your name?" Noor said. "I never asked."

"Choti. That's my name."

Noor widened her eyes. "Small? Your name is 'small?' I mean your real name, not some pet name."

Choti jumped to her feet to test out the slippers, parading around like a miniature police officer and repeating, "Choti, Choti, Choti."

Noor's eyes shifted around tracing Choti's heels as they marched in a circle of blurring blue, before she forced herself to look away.

"Are the slippers comfortable?" Noor said.

"Very. Thank you, Madamji," Choti said.

"So, small Choti, did you just invent your name?"

Choti stopped circumambulating Noor, rolled her eyes, and pointed out an emaciated dog lugubriously begging near a tea-stall. "Noor Madamji, do you see that dog?"

"Yes," Noor said, eying the dog as it continued to beg.

"What is that dog's name?" Choti said.

"I don't know, it's just some dog."

"Exactly," Choti's new slippers seemed to demand that she walk a few meters away from Noor before looking back, her eyes darkening. "The dog's name is just 'dog.' If the dog belonged to someone or was a pet jailed in someone's house, then it would either be collared with or sentenced to or limited by its name. Understand?" Choti said.

Noor stared at Choti, puzzled by the confidence of the small girl traipsing about in the slippers she had given her. "Sort of," Noor said.

"I used to live in a place called 'The Nameless House with Pink Walls.' No one had a name there, not even the owner of the house had a name. It would have defeated the purpose. There is safety in remaining without an identity, you know, you stay invisible, the police don't know who you are. We all look the same to everyone. We even called our guardian the 'Nameless Man,'" Choti said.

Noor shook her head and clicked her tongue at such a grand universal thought delivered with such innocence and insight by a child parading around her with the hubris of a god.

Satisfied she had test-driven her slippers enough, Choti walked back to Noor and sat down. "I'm still waiting to hear your name, Madamji…" Choti said.

Slowly a warm glow appeared in Noor's eyes. "I will tell you. Did you know that it was these ghats that gave birth to light?" Noor said, gently waving her hand in the air. "I was born amid these ghats. And when I was born, my grandfather named me 'Noor.' It means, 'light.' This birth of light is what the aarti is all about… "

Choti fell silent, then spoke. "I understand."

"You know what else, small girl?"

"What?"

"You know the Tulsi Ghat?"

"Yes."

"Where do you think it got its name?"

"Don't know."

"From the great poet Tulsidas."

Choti didn't know enough history to appreciate the amazing fact Noor had delivered to her ears. Instead, she jumped to her feet again to bounce on her blue toes and rock on her blue heels. "Noor Madamji, thank you so much for the slippers and for the story of light. I better get back to work or my friend Anarkali will have my hide for being late for our begging at the Chowk," Choti said. "Goodbye, and thanks for the slippers."

"Goodbye, child," Noor said. She watched Choti recede in a flash of blue slippers back into the maze of Varanasi's streets, a new light like a newly lit pair of aarti wicks flickering in her wizened eyes. She had wanted to tell Choti more about the story of light, but to take up the girl's time while committing the sin of trying to fascinate another human being seemed immoral. For the time being, Noor's story would have to wait. But she swore Choti had an even stronger bounce to her step than when she had first met the bold little tamasha-ist and beggar. As she stood, all Noor could do was sigh. She took the newspaper that had held the slippers and her water pot in her hands and returned to Ganga to complete her daily ritual for her tulsi.

Choti found Anarkali at her usual spot performing her usual routine—at Sangam Chowk.

Anarkali immediately noticed Choti's new slippers—they were too blue not to, and Choti was skipping around in them so blatantly, so how could she not?

"Well, hello, Miss *Mem*-sahib!" Anarkali said at the first sight of her.

"Like my new slippers?" Choti said, twirling around in her new shoes, radiant with happiness, "An old widow who is named after light gave them to me. Anarkali, did you know that light was born right here at the Varanasi Ghats? So, I suppose that means darkness was born here, as well."

Anarkali was too busy to immediately reply, and continued offering blessings or curses depending on her mood and her customer's categorization, into every window of every passing car. When she did take the time to reply, ceasing her begging to blink and roll her eyes, she said,

"Girl! Another misleading Hindu myth born of Varanasi. Who told you this nonsense? Light wasn't born *here*. Light was born of the sun, and the sun is far away, though with all the heat it beats us down with, I can see how someone might assume otherwise."

Choti walked toward a rickshaw to continue begging alongside Anarkali, stepping carefully to protect her new slippers, and threw her hands up in the air. "Anarkali, no!" Choti said. "This old widow, her name is Noor, said that light was born here on the ghats, and I believe her."

Anarkali sized up the couple Choti was begging from—Privileged Ones, no doubt—and said, "Choti, Varanasi is not a city of light, it is the City of the Dead, and it will always be the City of the Dead. There is only darkness here. Even a million aarti flames will never change that. Light? If light were born here, it would have been immediately cremated into Darkness." Anarkali became distracted and lurched over to intrude on the young man and woman Choti had snagged. "May you two stay healthy and together, and may you have as many beautiful sons as you desire," Anarkali confidently said.

Instead of smiling, nodding, and thanking Anarkali, the man's face flushed and his eyebrows furrowed in anger. "You ass, this woman is my mother."

Anarkali frowned and backed off. "Let's get out of here," the man commanded the rickshaw-puller, and the rickshaw sped away, the man turning to fix his glare on both Anarkali and Choti.

"Anarkali, you see?" Choti said, laughing. "Today your guesses and blessings and fortune-telling are all wrong."

Anarkali staggered over to sit down on the narrow sidewalk. "Choti, I know this old widow has filled you with the hope of Light, but the dark truth is that neither you nor me nor any of us out here on the streets really matter. I guess every man and woman who wants to have a boy ends up powerful and corrupt and with a potbelly and mustache like Raja—Choti such blinding bright blue slippers! Where did you steal them?"

"I didn't steal them, you haven't heard what I said, don't you like them?" Choti sat next to Anarkali and lifted her feet to show off her slippers' smooth blue soles.

"I was too busy working the traffic 'making a living' to compliment you properly. Where did you get them? Did you pull off another of your 'young-girl-with-sad-face' schemes?"

Choti jumped to her feet to strike a pose. "No, Noor, the old widow I told you about, gave them to me. She lives at the widow ashram at Bhoot Gali. Her grandfather was Tagore."

A scowl creased Anarkali's painted-up face. "Oh God, Choti, you need to learn more about life! It's inauspicious to talk to a widow like her. Widows are forever cursed, that is why they are forbidden from wearing celebratory colors and must remain in a constant state of mourning, dressed in no color other than white," Anarkali said.

Choti's jaw dropped.

"You had no idea, eh?" said Anarkali. "How old is this widow of light, this Noor? Tagore died almost a hundred years ago, so how could he be her grandfather? See? Even light has a dark side."

Choti became unsteady on her feet, especially for a bet-winning rope-walker who usually displayed excellent balance. "I don't believe it. She was so kind to me. Judging by the wrinkles on her face, she's at least a hundred years old herself. Anarkali, she was so nice to me and thoughtful enough to get me the blue—"

"Choti, I've heard enough. My advice is to avoid this 'widow of light' in the future," Anarkali said.

"Anarkali, let me ask you something," Choti said, changing the subject. "If you really have the power to curse people and kill them, do you think you could place a curse on all the lice in my hair and kill them, too, before they kill me first? They have me scratching so much that I can't concentrate."

"Cut your damn long hair if you want to get rid of your lice!" Anarkali fumed. "You're offering the little beggars a feast with all that hair!" Anarkali shrieked at a passing rickshaw for no reason other than to scare them. "Choti, I'm exhausted. You know I haven't made one single rupee since morning, every beggar in Varanasi seems to be visiting the ghats for aarti today. Damn little lights."

A couple of tourists chucked a half-eaten potato cutlet in Choti and Anarkali's general direction, and the two friends scooped it off the ground with their hands and blew off the dirt before squatting to devour it.

Choti frowned. "Anarkali. I will never cut my hair, lice or no lice. It's one of my powers in life. Never never never, and over my dead body," she said.

Anarkali stared at Choti, affection suddenly oozing from her eyes, smiling at Choti as she chewed.

THE BIRTH OF LIGHT

"Anarkali, where did you get your name?" Choti said between bites.

At first Anarkali didn't answer.

"Oh, come on, *na*," Choti said, raising her eyebrows and tilting her head, finally swallowing the big piece of potato cutlet she had been savoring in her mouth for as long as she could.

Anarkali continued to stare at Choti, before saying, "If you really want to know, I'll tell you."

Anarkali started her story:

"Once there was a Hindu couple who traveled from the region of Sindh, that would soon become modern-day Western Pakistan. The family was lucky to have survived the burning hatred of one of the largest massacres in India's history. The newly married couple, Aman and Sita, had left all their belongings in Sindh and were making one of the most challenging journeys of their life. Along the way, Sita had the thought she was pregnant, because she was vomiting and feeling nauseous. But Aman told her that they had to keep moving to stay safe. They needed to cross the border into India before the border was sealed.

"Back then, even in those days of chaos, betrayal, and mass killings, many still held to an ancient belief in the power of the pen. And that power had fully expressed itself when a line had been drawn between two nations that were in fact comprised of the same people. It was that simple line, drawn on a map by a human hand that caused so much sorrow and grief. A nation that might have been celebrating freedom and unity was left to mourn its division.

"Aman and Sita sought safety at refugee camp near Lahore. Afterward, they made the arduous train journey via Delhi to finally arrive at Varanasi. By that time, Sita's stomach had grown twice its size. Sita was right. She was pregnant.

"Being refugees, it was hard to survive, but they soon found work making bricks at a factory kiln that seemed as ancient as the Mohenjo-Daro site, which still bears the ruins of the ancient Indus Valley civilization. Nothing at the kiln—neither the bricks nor the attitudes of the boss and his workers—seemed to have changed over the centuries. Not one wind of freedom blew there for them, and everyone was a virtual slave. But, in order to survive and to be able to support their unborn child, Aman and Sita worked there alongside the many other families who had traveled the same path. They shared cramped shacks with the other workers, while turning the raw clay into the solid bricks that would build the New India.

"Months passed and Sita's stomach grew even larger, so large that it became too difficult for her to carry or cart the bricks going in and out of the kiln. A few months later, with the help of the other women at the kiln, Sita gave birth to what at the time everyone believed was a baby girl. Sita and Aman named their baby 'Lakshmi.' The reaction of almost all the people of the kiln was one or the other of two utterances: 'Next time it will be a boy,' or to console the new parents, 'Giving birth to Lakshmi will bring you good fortune.'

"But Sita knew something about her new Lakshmi was amiss. In the weeks following the birth, every time she gave her baby a bath, something stuck out that she wished she didn't notice and could simply forget. The thing tormenting Sita was a set of tiny male genitals that appeared just above Lakshmi's female folds. Lakshmi was not your average baby girl.

"Sita did not mention the anomaly to anyone and did everything she could to hide her naked baby from the eyes of her husband. She took to sitting alone atop the kiln's low walls, holding her daughter, while a million shaming voices screamed in her mind. She silenced the voices by holding her child as tight as she could for as long as she and her baby could hold their secret, but the tears that cleaned Sita's brick-dust and soot-covered face soon made a river that flowed strong enough for anyone to see.

"Sita felt as torn apart as the lands torn apart by the Radcliffe line. The division of Ardhanarishvara, the half-male, half-female form of Lord Shiva, was testing her. And the journey of accepting Lakshmi for what he or she was would prove even more difficult than her and Aman's journey from their native Sindh. Sita's mind reeled trying to find a solution. She could stop Lakshmi's breath before it felt the real air of life. She could do Lakshmi this favor of suffocation before the world saw her, knew her, or had the chance to do the same, which the world certainly would— or dishonor, reject, then discard her. Sita already felt the walls of prejudice, stigma, and pain Lakshmi would have to confront every day of her life closing in. Sita knew the sad life of the hijras of Sindh and she knew exactly where that life ended. Why allow a life only destined to end? These thoughts of dread gathered around her like the smoke she watched every day coming off the hardening bricks made from soft clay.

"When Sita went back to work, every day during breaks, she lightly rocked Lakshmi, whom she kept fully clothed in her cloth cradle, but was unable to rock away her thoughts of the harsh future her child was certain to face. The present wasn't any kinder to Sita, either. Even when mother and daughter became covered from head to toe with brick-dust and grime from the burning coals, Sita had to refuse to wash Lakshmi's body, lest she reveal the secret of her dual gender. The very thought of Lakshmi growing up was as repellent as viewing her undecided genitals. The prayers she had secretly made for the unity of her home nation, now divided by ink and brutality into nations, never sounded for the true gift she had birthed—a child possessing a unity of gender, who would have to forever live with the conflict of that unity. Sita saw no gifts from the gods or miracles coming their way.

"She was ashamed of it, but somedays Sita cursed the gods for delivering their rare 'gift' of Lakshmi to her. Other days she anticipated the day she would take Lakshmi and drown her in the Ganga. And when she wasn't anticipating that terrible act, she would dream about it, and she dreamed of Lakshmi's drowning many times.

"One afternoon, as Sita tried to balance herself as she carried a pile of bricks, a small poster stuck on the back wall of the kiln captured her eyes. It was a poster depicting Ardhanarishvara, him and herself:

THE BIRTH OF LIGHT

Half man, half woman
Half immortal, half human
Half giver, half receiver
Half becoming, half being
Half God, half Goddess

"Then Sita remembered the stories about Mohini, the female form of Krishna, her grandmother in Sindh used to tell her.

"As Lakshmi approached twelve years of age, the suspicion about her real gender increased so much amongst their community of refugee brick-makers at the Varanasi kiln that everyone forced Sita to reveal the truth.

"Within a matter of few hours of this revelation, Lakshmi suddenly became an outcast. There would be no place for her or her kind anywhere in their society. She was punished for a 'crime' she had no control over. If anything, it was a crime committed by God. Now Lakshmi was considered a curse. Sita's husband, Aman, became furious, betrayed by both God and his wife, and threatened to eject Lakshmi immediately from the kiln into the streets. The truth was that Sita was entirely disheartened, yet managed to remain strangely calm because she had other plans for Lakshmi. The wet clay-like, hopeful softness her heart had once felt even when reminiscing about Lakshmi's birth, the feeling of hope that had allowed her and her husband to travel the thousands of miles to find a new home after suffering a riotous division, had turned as hard as the bricks she and Aman now turned out at the kiln. Her heart was hard and dead, the joy of raising

Lakshmi, gone, the pain of keeping their secret, worse than ever.

"One day the small family of three decided to go see a tent-film together, going straight into the heart of Varanasi to watch *Mughal-e-Azam*, India's biggest silver screen epic of love, power, and betrayal. This was the first time the family watched a movie together, and it would be their last. Sita and Aman made it Lakshmi's happiest day, dressed her in her best pink frock and braided her hair in its usual two plaits complete with red ribbons.

"Lakshmi sat delighted and hypnotized in front of the big screen throughout, but when the movie ended and the lights came on she looked over and saw she was alone. Both her mother and her father had vanished. She sunk in her seat, waiting, but they never returned.

"The tent emptied and Lakshmi was left alone in total darkness. She ran out of the tent-theater and looked for her parents everywhere. They were nowhere to be found. She thought to go to the kiln the next day, but if they didn't want her, well, she decided she didn't want them either. Lakshmi began to cry. She loved her parents, especially Sita, but feared their punishment and humiliation. She braced herself, took a deep breath and went to live with other hijras such as she was in their community, and spent the rest of her days singing, dancing, cursing, blessing, and begging to survive. But for the rest of Lakshmi's life, she would never trust anyone again, and she had developed a serious love/hate regard for her once favorite film, *Mughal-e-Azam*."

Thus went Anarkali's tale, until Choti eagerly interrupted, "So, Anarkali, you are Lakshmi?"

Anarkali stared at Choti. "Before her parents abandoned her, Lakshmi loved the movie so much that, on that very day, she changed her name to 'Anarkali', the beautiful, ill-fated dancer from the film, who fell in love with a prince."

Choti fidgeted, listening, while Anarkali only persisted to stare at her. "But she also hated it so much for the moment it represented that she refused to ever watch *Mughal-e-Azam* or any other film again."

Whether anyone else cared to realize it or reckon with it or not, when Anarkali stood and begged in Sangam Chowk, in the reality of things, she stood at the crossroads of mortals and immortals, of male and female, of rivers and oceans. For the rest of Anarkali's life, she would burn and bake under Varanasi's unforgiving sun, as hot and ready as the hardened bricks that founded the free nation.

The Legacy of Nothing

What we leave behind and what we take

It was in the middle of the night, when Choti was in her sky nest looking at a constellation of stars in the heavens through the boughs of the tree she called home, that she heard muffled screams.

Choti looked through the small hole in her cardboard wall and saw two shadows fighting. One of the shadow's voices she recognized.

It was Anarkali.

"No, I won't open my mouth for—" she sounded desperate, like she was in pain. Choti recognized the other voice too, but it wasn't talking so much as making animal sounds. Then she heard heavy thuds like wood makes on flesh.

"Please, don't hit my arm again," was the last thing she heard from Anarkali's mouth.

Choti covered her ears and hid her face and head inside the bundle of old rags she used as her bedclothes. Having such a pillow was a luxury. She tried to sleep, but her mind wouldn't allow her to. The voices and activity she had listened to were too disturbing. To distract herself and calm herself to sleep, she peeked her head out from under the sarees to gaze at the lovely blue slippers Noor had given her. She knew it was weird for a person to sleep with their dirty slippers so close to their head, but their presence comforted her. Soon she fell asleep, wrapped in some bluish dream, she would never remember.

In the morning, even before her grunting cop alarm clock went off, she crept across the rooftop adjacent to the gym so she could be gone before the herd of teddy bear-killing animals arrived. She jumped off and walked briskly down the street in her blue slippers, headed for Anarkali's Temple of Fireflies—the name Anarkali had given her underground home. Anarkali didn't know she knew where she lived, but Choti knew a lot more than people gave her credit for.

Choti found the iron grill which Anarkali called her ceiling next to the manhole cover she called her front door. She knew exactly where to look through the grill to see if she was home. She knew every trace and shadow of Anarkali, so she could always tell even by the slightest movement if she was home. The slight amber-blue glow of early morning had started to fill the area, but Choti still didn't see or hear any trace of Anarkali, and that is what worried her.

Choti ran straight to Sangam Chowk, hoping to find Anarkali already working her turf: but she wasn't there either. That worried her even more.

Choti looked across the intersection toward Ram Sweets Shop and saw a group of people gathered in white kurta pajamas, the traditional Indian dress for men comprised of a loose-fitting long shirt and pants. Choti walked closer to Ram Sweets and saw Ram Halwai's son mounting his father's picture on the wall and draping a fresh flower garland around it. She knew what that meant: Ram Halwai had died.

Ram Halwai's son looked exactly like Ram Halwai, minus some years—whether or not the son also had a tap sticking from his belly, Choti didn't know and didn't want to. There were many things in life, she realized, that weren't meant to be known. *Is accepting this "not knowing" part of becoming a "grown-up"?* From what she had already seen and already knew, she already felt like one.

Ram's red money-box jumped out at her from the corner of his shop. Was it empty? Ram's belly had abandoned it, poor money-box. Ram Halwai had always held it so closely to his potbelly that the two seemed inseparable. The rupees they bred together inside the box seemed like their offspring, both betrayed and orphaned by Ram Halwai's departure. Choti wondered if the red money-box would have her, or if she could put it to use somehow. But that seemed wrong. How protective Ram Halwai had been about his shop, his sweets, his samosas, and his red money-box, and now he had suddenly left everything behind.

On the way to the ghats, Choti saw Noor in her plain white saree, which had collected more soot than usual. She was standing on a street corner staring at the colorful handprints—salmon-red, forest-green and corn-yellow—that certain of Varanasi's children had been allowed to press onto the wall with their traditional *abir* Holi color. The sight of Noor standing so still and staring off into space worried her. She seemed almost paralyzed with fascination, like the sight of so many hands had overwhelmed her. Then Choti saw something that really shocked her.

Noor looked around to make sure no one was watching—Choti didn't want Noor to see her spying on her, so she ducked behind a corner, but kept one eye on her—then she stepped closer to the wall, reached out her hand and placed it first on the red handprint, then on the green, and then on the yellow one. Then she backed away, looked around the area again, and walked away swiftly like she had never been there.

Instead of going directly to meet Noor at the ghats, Choti raced to the Nameless House with Pink Walls to pick up something special for Noor, something she recalled leaving there when she'd left. She was lucky the place was so dilapidated that the main gate couldn't even be locked. The angry cow was nowhere to be seen and everyone else seemed to be gone. Choti was able to rush in and rush out.

Minutes later, when she reached the ghats, Noor was already filling her brass pot with water from Ganga's shore. Choti knew on her way back up the steps she would see her if she sat down in the same spot on the crooked concrete steps where they had first met, so she did. What she really wanted to ask her was why she had pressed her hands against the colorful handprints at the wall, but she wasn't sure if she should. Pondering this question somehow took away her energy. Suddenly, Noor appeared next to her just as she thought she would. Choti was really deep in thought—this thought of wondering about old hands touching new color—because she hadn't even noticed her approaching, and now here she was.

"Noor, I've got something for you," Choti said.

Noor gently tapped her on the head. "You are younger than me, so it is only I who can gift you with something. That's the tradition," Noor said, and sat down next to her. She stared at her feet. "Speaking of gifts, I see from the fading blue of your slippers, you are making good use of the gift I gave you, daughter."

"Of course," Choti said. "I wear them everywhere; I would even wear them in my sleep, if I could."

Noor smiled, and Choti smiled back and looked at the palm of her hand she had absent-mindedly overturned. Her palm still showed a faint trace of colored abir. Noor seemed to notice her observing on her, because she quickly turned her palm down and wiped it on the cement and then on the underside of her white saree.

"Traditions are very important aren't they, Noor?" Choti said smiling sadly. "Tradition keeps everything in line."

"Yes, daughter, that's true," Noor said.

"My friend Anarkali said that you might be almost a hundred and fifty years old. Is that true?"

Noor grinned. "How did your friend get that idea?"

"Well, if Tagore was your grandfather, then—"

Noor laughed so hard it smoothed every wrinkle on her face and for a moment she almost appeared to be the same age as Choti. She could barely control herself, her body shaking, her stomach quivering as if it was the first time she had ever laughed and her body had no idea how to deal with the sensation. It was beautiful to watch. She seemed happier than anyone who had ever witnessed Choti's tamasha, and soon she was laughing and jumping around too.

Finally, Noor composed herself and stared and waved her skinny arms at Choti in order to stop her from calling so much attention to them—an old widow in colorless white and a grimy, orphaned street performer in fading blue slippers. *How dare they laugh together in public!*

"A thousand years old…" Noor laughed on softly as she shook her head. Then she got the hiccups.

"Oh!" Choti said. "Now the younger can help the older. Noor, mother, do what I tell you. Hold the tip of your tongue with your fingertips."

Noor was still racked with hiccups, but she did what Choti said. Choti's remedy worked and soon Noor's hiccups stopped. She sat down in relief. Choti didn't know whether it was her hiccups or laughter that did the most damage.

"Child, I must have forgotten what laughter even was. It almost broke me," she said. "And those hiccups."

Choti caught herself thinking about Anarkali again. She had no idea what had happened to her after the awful episode between her and Raja the previous night. Thinking of Anarkali immediately sobered Choti.

"Child!" Noor said. "We were just having so much fun and now you look so sad again. What happened?"

"It's nothing," I said. "Just a, uh, memory I had. Want to see what I got you?" I have been hiding the gift I had retrieved from the Nameless House with Pink Walls behind me for the whole time."

"Choti, I can't accept anything from you. It's not right, you are too young to give a thousand-year-old woman anything."

"Traditions are meant to be broken," Choti said and pulled Noor's gift out from behind her hip. "You like it?" she asked.

Noor went mute, but Choti could feel a pressure building up behind her lips and eyes as she stared at the gift to her: a discarded wig, of long, dark, silky, synthetic hair and a clean and lovely wig at that.

"Noor, friend, I went all the way to the Nameless House with Pink Walls, a place I ran away from, to get this for you. Someone who lived with me there who used to dress up like Durga wore it. I think it will look so pretty on you."

Noor gasped: "Child, you break every rule. I have no words for this." Noor didn't even reach out to touch her new head of fake hair, so Choti held it in her lap for her, hoping she would eventually accept it.

"You know that Ram Halwai died," she told her for no particular reason other than that it happened. Still, Noor said nothing. She just stared at the wig in Choti's lap, a small tremor riding from one corner of her mouth to the other and back again. "Noor, you got me something pretty for my feet and now I've got you something pretty for your head. We are even. If you accept it, I promise that younger will never give older anything ever again, not in a thousand years," Choti said earnestly.

Noor lifted her gaze to look her in the eyes. When their eyes met, hers seemed to melt, but Choti's lips held firm, unsmiling. "Noor, please," she said. "With all the years you've spent on earth, you deserve it."

Noor hesitated, but then gently slipped the wig from Choti's lap and buried it in her saree.

"Thank you for thinking of me," she said.

"Noor, what is your favorite color?" Choti asked suddenly, out of the blue.

Noor gasped again. "Color? What do I know about color? I haven't thought about color for such a long time. I barely know what to say about any favorite ones. My eyes wouldn't even know the difference between one or the other anymore. It's been such a long time since my husband died. Before that happened, I think it used to be pink, that deep pink at the bottom of a lotus flower, or the blushing cheek of a newborn child. Maybe that kind of pink, but like I said, I can barely remember," she said sadly.

At that moment, Choti knew that Noor thought about color more than she let on—but she decided not to press her about it because it might embarrass her and likely get her into some trouble. "Pink, huh?" is all she said. Then she stood up and ran away, leaving Noor to sit alone with her pretty new head of hair.

After Choti left, Noor made her way slowly through the jagged streets back to her ashram with her tulsi water and her wig. On the way, she passed the color-filled wall of hands but didn't even offer it so much as a glance. When she arrived, she opened the gate, snuck across the courtyard without looking at anyone and hoping no one looked at her. She did not water or circumambulate the tulsi plant. She went straight into the bathroom, locking the door behind her.

Noor went to the mirror with the wig Choti had given her, and, with her eyes closed tight, placed it on her head—for a moment she went numb at her own defiance. *How dare she! Such sacrilege!* Noor shivered and tugged the wig tightly into place and opened her eyes. *My God! She was young and beautiful again!* It was a perfect fit! *How could a poor, inexperienced child like Choti have known the wig would fit her old head so perfectly?* thought Noor.

Noor stared at herself in the mirror, almost against her will. The reflection was unrecognizable, but what she saw amazed her so much she almost fainted. But she couldn't dare faint, otherwise every other white-dressed widow, especially Asha, her roommate, would know what she was up to. Noor took a deep breath and stroked her neck and face and her stylish new head of hair with her fingertips, looking for all the world like the beautiful young married woman she once had been—her cheeks suddenly tinged with her favorite long-forgotten pink—a woman from another era, poised, elegant, coiffed, and cultured.

Noor couldn't help but beam as bright as an aarti flame at herself in the stained mirror, but when she did her heart beat against her ribs, racking her with guilt, and she tore the wig off to reveal that which she really was, or at least which she was destined by society to be: a luckless, pleasure-deprived, colorless widow.

Noor rolled up the wig, tucked it underneath her saree, and snuck into the ashram's kitchen to burn it in the wood-burning stove, as if she were cremating some lost part of her self.

After three days and nights of searching, Choti could not find Anarkali anywhere. Still deeply disturbed, on the fourth day, she relegated herself to beg alone on Sangam Chowk. The disappearance of first Chintu and now of Anarkali weighed heavily on her thoughts.

Suddenly across the stirring traffic she noticed Ram Halwai's son fighting with some authorities outside the shop. She had no idea what was going on, but even as she watched, the shop was boarded up, locked, and closed, leaving Ram Halwai's son slumped on the ground, only to suddenly stand and leave, his hands still covering his face. *Poor Ram Halwai's son*, thought Choti.

Choti had little enthusiasm for collecting rupees that day. It just wasn't the same without Anarkali. Not for the first time in her life, without her friend around, Choti felt lonely.

The next day Choti went to meet Noor at their usual place on the steps near the ghats. Choti sat down next to her, took out an old, pink-colored nail polish bottle and started applying it to her fingernails. Seeing Choti dabbing such a bright pink color on her fingertips brought the slightest of smiles to Noor's withered face.

"I had gone to Anarkali's house to look for her and found this. She loves this shade, she wears it all the time. Wearing it will make me feel closer to her," Choti explained, spreading out her pink-tipped fingers in front of her face and smiling at them. "Such a lovely color, don't you think?"

"Child, don't tempt me with this activity, if anyone sees me, they will kill me," Noor said, trembling. She let her eyes flutter from one of Choti's pink nails to the other. "It is such a lovely color. Like the bottom of a lotus petal."

Choti screwed the bottle of polish closed and frowned. "Noor, I can't find Anarkali anywhere. I've been looking for her for three full days," Choti said, and dropped her chin onto her hands.

Noor was so entranced by the color blooming at the ends of Choti's fingers that she didn't—couldn't—respond. Instead she reached down under her leg and pulled out her small pink book, then opened it and began to recite aloud some passages of Tagore, taken from his famous poem, *"Chitto jetha Bhayashunyo,"* "Where the Mind is Without Fear":

Where the mind is without fear and the head is held high
Where knowledge is free
Where the world has not been broken up into fragments
By narrow domestic walls
Where words come out from the depth of truth
Where tireless striving stretches its arms towards perfection
Where the clear stream of reason has not lost its way
Into the dreary desert sand of dead habit
Where the mind is led forward by thee
Into ever-widening thought and action
Into that heaven of freedom, my Father, let my country awake.

Even the words of Tagore couldn't distract Choti from her concerns about Anarkali. "Noor, I'm sorry, I want to listen, but I just can't. You don't understand. Anarkali has been with me like an older sister for almost three years. If I can't find her, I swear I will vanish too," Choti said, folding her arms across her chest and placing her fists crosswise under her armpits.

Noor closed her book. "Child, it's just a matter of time and Anarkali will appear again," Noor said. "She's older than you. She knows the Varanasi streets. I'm sure she is fine and knows how to handle herself. Take a deep breath."

Choti closed her eyes, leaned her head back and took as deep a breath as her worried little body could let in.

Noor shifted her gaze into the distance, over Ganga's ever-flowing waters. "You know, Choti, I told you before that as far as I could remember my favorite color was pink. But I've changed my opinion. Colors can divide people, especially here in Varanasi. Therefore, I feel that my favorite color must be the 'last' color."

"And what is the 'last' color, Noor?" Choti said, picking up her nail polish and brush and dabbing more color on her fingers, and then bending down to add color to her toes.

"The 'last' color is the color of ash," Noor said. "Ash is the color of every soul on its way to Nirvana, the color of every flame after it burns, the color of the oldest wisest eyes. At the end, everyone becomes the same, everyone becomes equal, everyone becomes identical, everyone becomes the color of ash. Nothing can divide this color, and this color divides nothing and no one. For me, the color of ash is the most beautiful color."

Choti dropped her nail polish brush and bent down to pick it up. The brush left a tiny dab of pink on the concrete

Choti, Chintu and Bhura with their rope.

(L to R) Rajesh, Anuj, Vikas and Neeraj after Holi in Vrindavan.

Choti and Chintu go for a drive and discuss what they want to be when they grow up.

Neena Gupta and Aqsa Siddiqui after their first acting workshop together.

Getting ready for the majestic Holi shoot.

(From L to R) Vikas, Bindu Khanna, Aqsa, Jitendra Mishra, Rajeshwar and Poonam Kaul during the shoot

Chintu on a bed of flowers.

Chintu counts his day's earnings.

Noor's roommate, Asha (Rashmi Sharma).

(From L to R) Bindu Khanna, Anuj Tyagi, Rudrani Chettri, Vikas Khanna, Rajeshwar, Neena Gupta, Aqsa Siddiqui, Jyoti, Aslam, Rajesh Singh and Subhransu Kumar Das.

The widows ashram before the Holi shoot.

Noor awash in her favourite color.

Noor and Choti in a tiny restaurant.

Widows line up to receive their daily rations.

Noor and Asha rehearse their lines.

Noor's room in the ashram.

The cast and crew at the final pack-up.

Chintu and Choti on the banks of the Ganga.

Noor steps out with her toes nails painted pink.

Noor braids Choti's hair.

Noor Saxena lights a lamp on the ghats of the Ganga.

Getting the perfect shot: Aqsa, Anuj, Vikas and Subhransu Kumar Das

Picture perfect: Subhransu and Vikas.

Noor praying to the rising Sun.

Gaay Ghat at sunrise.

Anarkali and Choti, learning the tricks of begging.

steps, like a small pink wound. She looked at Noor. "Well, that may be true, but I still prefer pink. Should I apply polish to your toenails?" Choti said.

Noor rebuffed Choti with a stern wagging of her finger. "Absolutely not! Widows are not allowed to touch color. It's a sin. I still remember when I was handed this piece of white cloth for the first time," Noor said, taking up the end of her saree. "I froze as the true meaning of it all sunk in. All my colored clothes were taken away from me and with that went my right to be happy, and as far as I was concerned, went my right to live and breathe."

Choti's only assessment of Noor's stubborn words was a lopsided smile. She poked a brush of wet pink polish on Noor's big toe. "Noor! Don't be silly," Choti said. "Allowing yourself one pink toe won't make a difference." Choti began to slather pink across Noor's yellowed and crusted toenail. Noor narrowed her eyes and became a detached onlooker to Choti's persistent bad influence. Choti's enthusiasm for being Noor's "bad influence"—how could a lovely color be a *bad* thing?—accelerated her polishing and within a minute, she had covered every toe of Noor's life-weathered left foot in glowing bright pink polish. The end result resembled a family of exotic birds perched on the stump of a mango tree, a sight Noor couldn't behold as she had tightly shut her eyes.

"There," Choti said. "Not the color of ash, but the color of many pretty toes." She screwed the brush back into the bottle of polish and shook it to stir the liquid up in order to attack the toes of Noor's right foot.

As she bent to apply pink to Noor's foot, the oversized boot of a police officer appeared in her frame of vision. Choti's frightened, open-eyed gaze scaled the boot, the potbelly that overhung the cop's belt, the cop's double-chin and past the cop's greasy mustache, to finally reach the summit of the cop's stern, unblinking sallow eyes. They were eyes whose dullness Choti recognized, the eyes of one of Inspector Raja's chamchas, merciless eyes that caused Choti to swallow hard.

The cop stroked his mustache. "*Aiii ladki*, hey girl, where is Anarkali?" Raja's goon intoned into Choti's face.

Choti's shoulders started to shake and Noor put an arm around her to calm her—she had already pulled her sinfully pink left foot under her white saree, away from the inspector's eyes.

"I've been looking for Anarkali too," Choti said, gulping in fear. "I have no idea where she is. I don't suppose you or your boss, Raja, would have any idea, would you?"

The policeman raised his stick. "Shut your mouth, girl!" he shouted this time, sending Choti scrambling off the steps in the direction of Tulsi Ghat, and the chamcha in hot but bumbling pursuit.

Now alone, Noor stared at something on the concrete steps. In the chaos, the bottle of nail polish had tipped over, spilling its pink contents. *Run and hide Choti and don't let them catch you! We will find each other later*, Noor wanted to shout, but couldn't muster the courage, and Choti did not turn back. Instead, she was racing through the Varanasi maze, and soon enough easily escaped Raja's chamcha. *A potbelly always runs out of breath before a rope-*

walker, she thought, as she arrived, panting, near Tulsi Ghat, still puzzled over what had happened to Anarkali, although Choti surmised that Raja and his chamchas already knew that she knew exactly what had been transpiring in their gym those late nights after she had ostensibly fallen asleep.

Noor reached the ashram, deeply troubled and feeling a little dizzy. As she crossed the courtyard, she lowered her eyes, and when she did, they were sent blinking into shock: her toes displayed traces of the color Choti had applied! Pink painted toes flitting across an austere courtyard of a white widow's ashram? *What was she thinking? Had she gone mad?* She couldn't dare be seen with such bright pink-painted toenails, it was a sin, an unforgivable offence and if the other widows were to find out they would throw Noor out.

Noor quickly lengthened her white saree, tugging at the folds to hide her left foot. That way she could water and circumambulate the tulsi as usual. Then she snuck into the bathroom to wash her toes of any trace of nail polish, scrubbing until her toes hurt. But the nail paint wouldn't wash off. She scraped at it with her nails and managed to rip off some bits but couldn't get rid of it all. She lengthened the folds of her saree and scrunched her toes under it and went straight to her room, where she collapsed onto her sheets and wept like a child.

Asha happened to be sitting outside their room on the balcony. Asha was sure to have heard Noor crying, but whether she had just witnessed any of Noor's other behavior, Noor didn't know. All she knew was she'd have to be very careful not to let anyone catch a glimpse of her toes.

In the morning, Choti awoke in her sky-nest still wearing her blue slippers. She immediately slid down the boughs of her tree to circle back to where she had fled from the day before, but this time she chose to peek from around a corner so none of Raja's watchful chamchas would witness her searching for Noor again. The new morning's search proved easy because Noor was already sitting in the same place, waiting for her like she had never left, and even from a distance, Choti's hawk eyes could see that the pink polish she had applied to Noor's toenails, was still peering out from under her saree, as shamefully vibrant as the day before—though she wasn't wearing the wig Choti had given her.

Choti whistled to get Noor's attention, then waved the widow over to a more discreet place around a sharp, hidden corner along the ghat's terrace. Choti knew every hidden corner along the ghats' fringes, and she could not afford to be seen.

When Noor finally appeared around the corner, she saw Choti splayed out, sitting dejectedly on the ground, flies buzzing around her face and dark patches of purple swirling about her eyes. The poor girl had finally become exhausted, and she was babbling into the air at no one, on the verge of panic. Noor kneeled beside her and placed her old gnarled hand on Choti's forehead. "Child, what happened to you?" Noor said.

"I am talking to the ghosts," Choti said. "I am not scared of you, ghosts, I am scared of real people. Ghosts are pure energy, so why would they ever have to wear a mask? And living people wear so many masks, they can't be trusted to keep the same face on very long. Do I trust the eternal ghosts of the dead, or the changing masks of the living?"

"Child! You're not making any sense, poor thing, take a breath and calm down," Noor said.

"Not making any sense?" Choti said. "Consider my 'friend' and tamasha 'partner' Chintu. He stole all of our hard-earned money and kept it for himself. His mask changed. First it was clever, trustworthy, and always smiling, then suddenly it became stupid, unreliable, and ugly. I should have known his mask would eventually change from all the times he went to Manikarnika to push his greedy fingers into the ashes of the dead for their belongings. He had me doing it too. Now I hate what I did, people should be allowed to take what they love with them. With Anarkali gone missing, whom can I trust?"

Noor cocked her chin. "You can trust me," she said. "You can trust me."

"I hope that's true," Choti said. "Because, as you saw, Inspector Raja is starting to send his chamchas around to threaten me. I want to fly, but if I can't fly, I would rather be a reliable ghost than become an untrustworthy, mask-changing, human being."

"One day you will fly, mark my words," Noor said, stroking the side of Choti's face, and smiling down at her as if Choti was—*curse the very thought!*—her own newborn. "Child, you are too young to realize it yet, but you are stronger than all these people who hide behind their changing masks."

Choti sat up to stare along Ganga's shore to the ghats further toward the Ganga Mahal Ghat, where in the hazy distance she could see many people setting their aarti lamps aflame. "Noor, why do people light these lamps all day long, even in the daytime?" she said.

"You don't know?"

Choti shook her head.

"I will tell you. There are two types of lamps to be lit for aarti. The first one is lit to make a wish. The second is lit when that wish is fulfilled," Noor said.

Choti perked up. "Did you ever light your wish lamp?" she said.

Noor nodded and suddenly glared at her hands, "Destiny!" she said, then shifted her glare to Choti, where, resting on Choti's innocent wide eyes, her gaze softened. "I lit a wish lamp only once, and that was long ago, when I was married. My grandfather never wanted me to get married. He was heavily influenced by the independence movement and social reforms. He would say that the only way our country could progress was to educate girls. For a woman, not getting married went against everything our culture stood for, so, of course, no one respected my grandfather's defiant, open-minded hopes for his granddaughter to remain single. Do you know how old I was when I got married?"

Choti shook her head.

"I was even younger than you," Noor said. "Only nine or ten years old when I was married off. After I was married I went to the Sangam—"

Choti, eager to know more about Noor, interrupted, "The Sangam Chowk?"

"No, child, the Sangam of Rivers," Noor said. "A very sacred place a few miles from the Chowk, the place where Ganga Ma and Yamuna Ma meet the very special Saraswati Ma," Noor said. "I went with my husband and family to light the first lamp, and that lighting happened to occur on the day my elderly husband suddenly passed away."

"I don't know the Saraswati," Choti said, her ears burning with curiosity.

"And you wouldn't, because the Saraswati isn't visible to the human eye," Noor said. "It's only visible to the mind."

"—I feel like the Saraswati Ma, you know why?" Choti said.

Noor only stared.

"Because I am also invisible. I can prove it because somedays when I'm knocking for rupees on car windows, no one sees me. When that happens, I don't want to be invisible. But I wish I could be invisible like the Saraswati when the police-wallahs come looking for me."

Noor nodded. "I understand. I also feel invisible many times. But to me this is neither good nor bad, it just is."

"Noor?"

"Yes?"

"What did you wish for when you lit your lamp at the Saraswati Ma?"

"It's a long incomplete story, do you want to hear it?" Noor said, and Choti nodded.

Noor took a breath, and spoke. "That day, in 1930, when the bells of the Krishna temple rang along the Asi Ghats was no ordinary day. It was Janamashtmi, the day of the birth and continual rebirth of Lord Krishna, who many consider their favorite god, though as a child he was said to have stolen everyone's butter. Krishna was a musician, a lover, a friend, a statesman, a philosopher of the *Bhagvad Gita*—the very song of God—and he was also very mischievous, which made Janamashtmi itself a day of potential mischief.

"That day in Krishna's temple, while a huge congregation of devotees were singing hymns to their favorite god, an excitable man named Dwarka pulled at the rope of a small cradle with a small idol of Krishna attached to it. Sometimes another devotee, some friend of Dwarka's, would relieve Dwarka of his dutiful rope-pulling ceremony, but Dwarka would eagerly push his friend out of the way to go back to rocking the cradle of Lord Krishna.

"This was Dwarka's big day, because, back home, his wife was helping their only daughter deliver a child, his new grandchild, and he expected that at any moment someone would enter the temple with the good news. As the temple bells deafened everyone with their beautiful echoing tones, a man rushed to Dwarka to whisper in his ear. 'Bauji, Bauji, it's—a girl…'

"Dwarka stopped pulling his cradle-rope and shouted, 'Radhay! Radhay!' becoming so excited that he dropped the rope altogether and started dancing with the other devotees.

"The whispering message-bearer chased Dwarka into the dancing throng to deliver the other news he had, but Dwarka was impossible to catch as he danced and clapped, too excited to keep to the beat, as his thanks to the gods for answering his prayer. Finally, the news-bearer found Dwarka's ear and placed his lips close to the joyous new grandfather's mouth, '…but your daughter passed away after giving birth.'

"As morning broke the next day, after an exhausting night of warring emotions, Dwarka shuffled home through streets strewn with a carpet of flowers, remnants of the previous night's Janamashtmi celebrations. It was the mischief part of Krishna's day that got Dwarka wondering if his new granddaughter had been born healthy. He picked up his pace across the flower petals to rush home through the narrow, unawakened streets of Varanasi to find answers to the many questions on his mind. *Who would take care of his little Radhay? What would the future bring?*

"Dwarka entered his home through a pink door decorated with auspicious symbols.

"Nearing the main entrance of his home, Dwarka felt the pain of seeing his daughter's corpse lying in their courtyard, draped in a red saree, her nostrils stuffed with cotton and her eyes closed in peace. A vermilion swath covered her forehead, which symbolized she had died a married woman…"

"I've seen many dead women, some of the corpses even have full makeup on," Choti piped in, interrupting Noor's story.

Noor smiled sadly. "Well, Dwarka barely saw his daughter, instead he saw a little girl near his cowshed swaddled in old rags and crying out in hunger. Dwarka rushed over to hold Radhay, his new Krishna baby, in his arms, unable to tear his eyes from her. And then a miracle happened. A ray of morning light suddenly shifted to Radhay's face. She became radiant, her eyes shimmered, her smile sparkled even though she had no teeth, and her still, previously folded hands started to reach toward Dwarka, already exercising their free will.

"It was as if the sun had risen just to kiss her and send its rays to caress her downy hair. The sight of her melted Dwarka's heart, and the worrying he had done over the newborn child disappeared. This tiny being, his new granddaughter, a girl of Krishna himself, could even wake up the sun! Then and there, Dwarka changed her name from Radhay to 'Noor'—'Light,' the light of eternity, the light of survival, the light of new hope. The sun's light made Noor's fragile body almost translucent, as if lit from within, like a candle under glass, or a firefly."

Choti cleared her throat.

"Are you bored of my old widow's tale, child?" Noor asked. Her voice had become slightly hoarse. Her eyes were moist with remembering. Choti was scared she might cry, and wanted to change the subject. She stammered, "Not at all, I just feel like my heart wants to leap out through my throat."

Noor sighed deeply. "Okay, I'm getting tired, anyway. If you enjoyed my story, and I can ever remember the rest of it, I will tell you more another day," Noor promised.

THE LEGACY OF NOTHING

"It's a deal," Choti said, and then yawned as if she had just awakened from a dream.

The next day they were back at their old haunt.

Noor looked at the brightening sun and closed her eyes against its rays. "Choti, everything is going to be okay. Anarkali will come back. The Saraswati Ma running through my heart tells me so," she said.

Choti stood up sleepily, sighed, and braced her shoulders like she did when she was walking her rope. "Noor, you know, I sleep above an open gym where these thuggish police wrestlers arrive in a grunting herd to wake me up every day. You see the dark circles around my eyes?"

Noor nodded. "I do," she said.

"I can't get any sleep because I've heard them in the night. I've also heard Anarkali's schemes. I'm not stronger than those beasts, Noor, and I can never hope to be," Choti said. She scratched violently at her head. The lice were becoming hungrier and more vicious. "Uff! Speaking of animals, these little beasts are starting to eat me alive."

Noor's eyes darted from Choti's now quivering lips to the top of her head. "Girl, I know how to get rid of your lice. I have a special oil to kill them. I will bring it with me next time."

They sat quietly for a while and then Choti suddenly grabbed Noor's hand and started to pull her along in the direction of Tulsi Ghat. "I know of this great chai-stall in your grandfather's ghat. You must like tea, and this place I have in mind is a place no one will ever find us," Choti said, accelerating with the energy of the child she really was and almost pulling Noor off her ancient, 1000-year-old pink-encrusted feet.

"Choti! Slow down," Noor protested. "If we go to a public place to have chai, someone is certain to see me. And it will be particularly terrible for us to be seen together. Better to stay here and forget the chai."

Choti wouldn't let up and kept pulling Noor along beside her. "Noor, that's silly. Don't you remember? No one will see us because we are invisible," she said, and then undid the small knot tied into the end of her frock to retrieve some coins. She looked at Noor. "One day I want to have a proper frock with a proper pocket instead of a loose, ragged knot. Then I can finally do all my business properly."

Choti led Noor onto a terrace hidden in a secluded section of Tulsi Ghat that gave way to an almost paradisaical 360-degree view of every ghat flowing down to Ganga like variations on a stone waterfall. City of the Dead? From there, it wouldn't have been too far off for the viewer to regard Varanasi as the "City of The Living," and in the sixty years of Noor's patient and humble water-getting routine along the same well-worn path, it was a panorama that she had never pleasured her eyes with, one she was even too ashamed to please them with now.

The revitalizing view ended at the chai stall of Choti's mention. The traditional chai-vendor's cart was a simple affair with an earthen stove and an old steel kettle, served in Varanasi's signature sun-baked earthen cups, whose sides sometimes had intricate designs carved into them, as well as plastic jars full of dark chai leaves, sugar, and small packets of cardamom.

Choti dragged Noor to the cart. "Bhaiya, two cups tea. Extra extra sugar," Choti confidently said to Sonu, the chai-wallah, who was dressed in a faded long blue kurta with a red scarf tied around his head. "For my special guest," she said, tossing a glance back at Noor, who hung sheepishly behind.

The vendor eyed the strange couple: a little kid and an old widowed woman, as he steeped the chai in boiling water and strained it through an old sieve. Soon the early air of spring filled with the fresh, rustic aroma only a cloud of fresh chai steam can produce.

Choti stared at Noor, smiling in anticipation of the pleasure she knew the tea would bring to poor Noor's long-neglected palate.

The vendor narrowed his gaze at Noor as he dumped large heapings of sugar in both of their chais. The more he stared at the old widow, the more his face grimaced with repulsion. It was a repulsion Choti noticed, and so she grimaced right back. "Just serve your chai, Sonu, and don't act so smart," said Choti. She flipped the vendor his rupees and snatched both the teas from his cart, not giving the man the courtesy of even one more word of thanks, as she tossed her head, and handed Noor her steaming cup of sweet tea.

The two new friends walked toward an old bench that promised the best view of the Ganga and all that she symbolized. The light wind that blew in whispered rumors only the winds of Varanasi could spread—the harsh stories of survival amid the softer stories of Ganga, and how both expressed themselves across the oldest city of humans, the city that had the power to break the cycle of life and death.

When Choti and Noor sat down on the bench, Noor finally pulled her saree away from her head and whiffed at the fragrant steam rising from the earthen chai cup. She looked at Choti and smiled. Something about the aroma seemed to elevate her soul.

Choti eagerly sipped at her chai. "Noor of the Light, did Sonu put enough sugar in your chai?" she said, before interrupting herself to say, "Do you even like sugar? It is white after all."

Noor only smiled. She held the earthen cup in her hands, relishing its warmth coming through, and nodded. "Child, I had forgotten how sugar tastes. It's been so long, my tongue doesn't know how to react, or whether sweetness has become the taste of salt," Noor said.

"I'm sure your tongue will get used to it," Choti said.

"Perhaps," said Noor. "My grandfather had a mango tree in his yard. And every spring I used to eat the unripe still-green mangoes. Somehow the taste of these sour mangoes became my favorite taste. But I've forgotten that taste too, what with my fifty to sixty years of only eating plain rice. This is why I have no idea what to say about the sweetness of this chai, what it tastes like, or how it makes me feel. It's all very confusing."

Noor took tentative sips and let the taste linger in her mouth—Choti could tell because after every sip, Noor pursed her lips and puffed out her cheeks. Ganga's serene natural breeze seemed to have blown away most traces of Noor's guilty pleasure, yet her smile still fought to remain on her face.

It wasn't too long before, perhaps propelled by that same Ganga breeze, the inevitable swarm of Varanasi flies came around, attracted by the sugar-sweetened chai. One fly after another arrived to buzz around Noor, and some even spun down to buzz and rub their legs together and stare with their red eyes, atop the rim of her cup. One fly flew right into it, landing on the chai's frothy surface, and had the gall to swim about! Choti quickly flicked it out with her stirring stick.

"Bloody little beasts. If it's not Chintu, it's Raja's chamchas, if it's not Raja's chamchas, it's lice, if it's not lice, it's these bloody flies," Choti said. "I'll keep them away so you can enjoy your chai."

Choti spent the rest of her time with Noor happily waving away any fly that dared approach to bother Noor or land anywhere near her cup as she drank her chai. And with every tender, caring wave of Choti's arm, Noor's eyes moistened a little more, though she never let on how much the simple gesture meant to her.

"Did you ever go to school?" Choti asked her new friend as she waved her arms to shoo away the flies.

"No, I didn't. I wasn't allowed to, it wasn't my place," Noor said.

Choti smiled. "Anarkali doesn't like tea, but she loves the milk that goes into it. Chintu loves the sugar! He is always stealing sugar whenever he can; sometimes he eats it straight from his fist! Dirty thief! No wonder his teeth are so bad." Her voice grew suddenly wistful: "Noor?"

"Yes?"

"If you have to go somewhere, please let me know, don't disappear on me like..." she stopped abruptly and looked away.

Noor put her hand gently on Choti's head and stroked it. "No, meri Choti, I promise." She put her arm around Choti's thin shoulders.

"Noor?"

"Yes, child?"

"That pink book that you always have with you..."

"Yes? What about it?"

"You can read it, right?"

Noor smiled sadly. "I can read a little but I'm forbidden to. It would give me too much pleasure. My grandfather wrote these Tagore quotes and poems in my book when I was a child. I try not to actually read them, I just remember them word-by-word from memory. Please don't tell anyone."

"I will never tell anyone, I promise. But Tagore *was* your grandfather, right? Anarkali didn't believe me bu—"

"—Child! I wasn't being serious," Noor interrupted before Choti could finish her sentence, and then hit her forehead with the flat of her hand. "Tagore isn't my *actual* grandfather. Because I recite his poems every day of my life, he has *become* more like my spiritual grandfather. The real Tagore was a writer who lived in Calcutta and died soon after I was married. My real grandfather was a great admirer of his. Tagore's not related to me, but has always remained close to my soul."

Choti nodded and giggled. *"Oh teri!* You were making a joke! Like a fool, I thought Tagore was your real grandfather and that he lived a thousand years ago, so I thought you were somehow immortal, or at least hundreds of years old," Choti said, now grinning broadly with a sparkle in her eyes.

"My grandfather was also a great poet, he would often tell me that even Ganga Ma flows towards Tagore's house every day to hear his poetry," Noor said, involuntarily lifting her chin with a vague pride.

"Yes, but your grandfather was not Tagore?" Choti said, shooing away more flies as Noor sipped and swallowed her last drops of chai.

"No," Noor said. "No, dear, he was not."

Noor entered her room and, suddenly, without warning, overcome with all that was happening in her life, broke down into unending tears.

Asha entered the room a short while later and stood over her with her arms crossed. "Noor, what's happened? I haven't seen you cry once, let alone like a river, in the fifty years I've known you. Did someone say something cruel to you? Do something terrible to you? Insult you? I don't know what's gotten into you, but I can't stand seeing you weep like this."

Noor sat up, covered her feet, and reached for Asha to give her a hug, her tears still flowing as openly as the Ganga. "Asha, can you believe I had chai earlier today?" Noor said. She brought the back of her hands to her face and started to wipe away the tears clinging to her cheeks.

Asha pulled out of Noor's desperate hug and grabbed her by the shoulders. "What? *Ram Ram*," Asha chanted, for the Lord Rama's forgiveness on behalf of Noor.

"And a fly flew into it," Noor said.

"Oh! Did you put too much sugar in it? Ram Ram. What's *wrong* with you?" Asha said, her already stern voice becoming sterner. "Noor, have you forgotten where you live? This is Varanasi. There are as many flies here as there are ashes. They are everywhere and you are acting like it was the first time you ever saw one. It landed in your chai? That's why you are crying?"

Noor's breath heaved and spluttered. "No, no. She—the child—she shooed away all the flies, so I could drink my chai in peace," Noor said.

Asha stood back in shocked disapproval. "Noor, what's gotten into you?" whispered Asha.

Noor shook her head from inside the pallu of her saree.

"Why are you having chai with someone in the first place? Especially a poor needy child? You know women like us aren't allowed to do such a thing."

Noor took a deep breath. "Asha, you don't understand," Noor said. "It's not about the flies or the sugar, this is the first time in my life someone thought about me before they thought about themselves. Do you understand?"

Asha started to writhe with fury. "Ram Ram," she said, even more stern than before.

"This is the first time in my life, Asha, that I feel like I have…a daughter. Now I want to color myself in pink, bright Rajasthani pink…"

"Shut your mouth! Don't dare say that! For a colorless widow to become attached to a child like she's your own rosy flesh and blood daughter is the lowest of sins! Have you forgotten who you are and why you have to live at the ashram with the rest of us? You are a widow, you are meant to live plainly and colorlessly without anything, and when you die, you are not allowed to leave anything behind—*mahadev ki marzi*. This is Lord Shiv's edict. You must not become attached to anyone else on this earth. If you do, you are certain to rot in hell when you die," Asha said, as she furiously paced their room.

Noor turned her face away to stare through her drying tears at the empty void of the balcony. A breeze blew into the room but offered no relief or pleasure. "I have been rotting in hell while I live," were the only words Noor could think to say.

The Lost Spring

From imaginary homes to illusory colors

Inspector Raja arrived home drunk on his motorbike in the middle of the night. The quieting growl of his bike's engine was still loud enough to wake his wife, Rani.

Raja parked his bike and stumbled into his house. His mother lay on a charpoy in the front room, "Do you know why your darling wife hasn't borne you a son even after bathing in Lolark Kund every day?"

Even though Raja ignored his mother, she said, "Someone told me she goes down all the steps but doesn't so much as wet her feet in the sacred water."

Rani was heating up Raja's usual meal as the drunken inspector plowed through the kitchen door and listed toward his wife like an overladen Ganga dinghy, his breath foul and pungent enough to dowse any flicker of Rani's usual greeting smile. "I don't want any dinner!" Raja shouted.

Rani turned her head away and clasped her hands together at the waist of her saree. "But Ji, I made your favorite dish—Banarsi aloo curry…"

Raja listed closer: "Rani, you can't ever give me what I want! You hear me?" he said.

Rani rushed to the bedroom door and quietly closed it. "Shh! Raja! The girls are asleep, they have school tomorrow," she said.

Raja grabbed his wife roughly by her shoulders: "I don't care if they never go to school. You realize, I can stop your daughters' schooling any time I want? You should know that," Raja said, waving his finger threateningly in her face.

Rani's eyes were lowered, but she stood taller. "Raja, calm down, I beg you."

"I won't," Raja roared. "How many times has my mother asked you, even begged you, to go to Lolark Kund so we can finally have a son?" Raja said. "And now she's telling me that all these years, you have never even touched the water?"

"Raja! You're drunk. Can we discuss this tomorrow? The girls need their sleep for school."

"Rani, how many times?" Raja repeated, his eyes bloodshot, "how many times did I beg you? How many times did my mother beg you, even try to set an example for you? All I want is a son and you bitch, you never gave me one! Why do you have to torture and humiliate me?"

On nights like this, when Raja arrived home drunk and bitter, she had to question everything her mother had taught her about remaining silent for the sake of peace. To be silent was to accept, to bow, to give up. It was only for the happiness and stability of her daughters' lives that Rani would not reply.

Like her husband, Rani came from a family of police officers, a family who lived in a village near where Raja was born. Unlike her husband, Rani was educated and had graduated high school, while Raja had to pay to get a school certificate. Her husband was born late to his parents, twenty years into the marriage of Shiv, his policeman father, and Nandini, Raja's mother—and it had taken year after year, prayer after prayer, ghat after ghat, and priest after priest for Nandini to finally conceive her precious boy: Raja, stubborn, entitled, obnoxious Raja.

When a son is born late in his parent's marriage, to parents already softened by decades of waiting, chances are the boy grows up rarely hearing the word "no." This explained a lot to Rani about her husband's pugnacious attitude. He was a loud, demanding, hostile "mama's boy," but one whom Rani still tried to love. Was it entirely her husband's fault that the same shadows and condemnations his mother experienced from her in-laws and husband, still chased and taunted him?

Early in their marriage, Raja's mother, Nandini, educated her on how a woman should always seek to please her in-law's family day-in, day-out, especially her husband. She told Rani to always have fresh hot rotis on the table. Though she did her best, Rani found her cooking always being faulted and her behavior constantly judged by Raja and his parents, and she found Nandini's relentless speeches about how food should taste, or who was the better cook, Nandini or she, deeply annoying.

And every time Rani touched the feet of an elder of Raja's family, they always blessed her with the same statement, "*jaldi jaldi beta do,*"—give us a son quickly. Her twin purposes in life seemed to be ensuring a constant supply of those hot, puffed, ghee-buttered rotis into Raja's mouth, and becoming some sort of son-birthing machine. Rani's own desires in life were totally irrelevant. "Husband is God. Obey Him. Your Husband's in-laws are more important than your own family. Revere and worship them," Her mother-in-law said over and over.

Rani had to suppress her own achievements, her dreams, her personality, to enter Raja's family's bounds. They saw no value in education, no real value in being a woman. Every time she and Raja had an argument related to her daughters' attending school (which was often) Raja's contention was that educating a girl was a waste of money. "What good is an education for cleaning the house, washing clothes, or cooking dinner?" he would say. At which Nandini, if she happened to be there, would whisper, "*Ek chup sau sukh,*"—Only in silence is there peace—basically asking Rani to shut her mouth and surrender.

Ten years of marriage to her husband had produced three daughters, two miscarried boys, and no sons for Raja. Every time Raja arrived home stinking of liquor and the dirty money he had earned, Nandini's voice would rise up like a djinn from the fumes of his foul breath to remind Rani how she, Raja's mother, in order to give birth to her own son, had bravely visited Lolark Kund at least four times every month.

Did no one realize that, after two miscarriages, it was medically dangerous for Rani to try to birth a son for Raja? She would have to risk her life! Now as she tried to calm her drunk husband, she heard his mother's words louder than ever, "So many times I left my earrings or bangles in the well at Lolark Kund to please the Gods enough to grant my dynasty a son who will carry forward our family name and legacy."

Then Rani recalled the day that had infuriated her the most, not only because of her husband's misbehavior, but because, always the submissive wife, she had said not one word in protest. Her three daughters, Sita, Durga, and Saraswati, whom Rani had named for her three favorite Hindu goddesses, had come home early that day in order to proudly tell their father what they had been excelling at in school.

"Papaji! I scored 88% on my government studies test, but I wish I had focused more on mathematics, and then I could be at the top of the class," said Sita, Rani's eldest. Durga said: "Papaji! I am the top dancer in my 5th grade dance class, and next year I plan to be at the top of my 6th grade dance class, too," the middle one said. Then Saraswati, the youngest one said, "Papaji! My teacher told me she is so proud that I'm the best mathematician in my math class—she even took me to see my Principal Ma'am, in her office so she could congratulate me. And you know what Ma'am said?" Raja didn't even look up from his paper. "She said I was her favorite student in the whole school and if I set my mind to it, I could become anything I wanted to be—even an astronaut!"

Raja didn't look up, so the little girl tugged at his sleeve. "What is it?" Raja had finally bristled, squinting his eyes and trying to shut out the image of Saraswati floating around in space proclaiming to the universe that she was her father's daughter—the *third* of *three*.

"What do you want me to be, Papaji?" the young astronaut-to-be had asked then.

"I don't want you to become *anything*," he'd shouted at the shocked girl. "Become a son, can you do that?"

Rani could have slapped his face. The manner in which Raja and his family treated her daughters as insignificant—only good for becoming future roti slingers and son-makers—suffocated her. Their education wasn't necessary, their development not a priority, their health and well-being insignificant.

Rani's darkest truth was that, beyond the medical risks, she was terrified of giving birth to a son because she was certain he would turn out just like Raja, for Raja was just like his own father. How far does a fruit fall from the tree? Rani was determined more than ever to give her daughters the best education she could, even if she had to suffer through Raja's drunken evening rages.

The commotion had awakened their slumbering daughters. Rani could hear them moving restlessly in their sleep. When Rani reached out to pacify her husband, Raja barreled into the bedroom he shared with her and crashed onto their mosquito-netted wooden bed, still in his uniform and boots, and still holding his baton.

Rani followed him in to at least relieve her husband—and their always crisply sheeted bed—of Raja's street and tavern-soiled boots. When Raja felt his daughter-bearing wife's hands yanking at his boots, he reached down and pushed her away, then sat up to push her away with more force.

THE LOST SPRING

"Raja! You're soiling our bed with your dirty boots! Take them off!"

Raja kicked off his boots and rolled over onto his back. "Rani, Ma told me you never go far down deep enough when you bathe at Lolark Kund. You go down the steps but never into the water. Everyone saw you," Raja said.

Rani sat by her husband's head on the edge of the bed. She stared into her husband's drunken eyes like a mother might stare at her misbehaving son. "Raja, listen," Rani said. "You and I are blessed with three beautiful daughters. They are like having our very own aarti lamps at home, all the time. The light they bring us every day makes us truly blessed."

Raja turned his back to her. "I don't want them, you can have them. If you don't return to Lolark Kund and take a proper dip in the holy waters, I will find another wife who will give me a son," Raja growled. Soon the ferocious rasping of his snores further sullied his wife's ears.

It was pointless.

Rani stood up, turned off the bedroom lights on her drunken husband, crossed the kitchen, and went to sleep between her precious daughters, embracing them all and whispering into their ears the same words she'd whispered to them after the astronaut incident: *Be anything you want my dears, be who you are, be yourself. Bring a revolution. Fly.*

Choti walked the narrow streets behind the Tulsi Ghat, passing stall after stall stacked with mounds and packets of every possible shade of Holi pigment. The pigments were not things she felt she could touch, for Holi was not a holiday for invisible, colorless scums-of-the-earth like Choti and Anarkali, and certainly not for a widow like Noor.

At the end of the kaleidoscopic gauntlet of dazzling colors, Choti spied a cart full of *ambis*—green, tart, tangy unripened mangoes—and she remembered how Noor had said she loved them. When Choti tried to speak civilly to the mango-wallah about his mangoes, the vendor only glared down his gourd-like nose at her and crossed his arms. "What do you want, street girl? Get away from my cart, *shoo*. You are scaring my customers away," he said.

Choti glared back into the vendor's face and ground her teeth, and before the mango-wallah could do anything about it—*has his nose obscured his vision?* Choti had to wonder—she snatched a pair of the fattest ambis her eyes could find and ran as fast as her legs could carry her. If only she could have run so fast earlier, she might have caught that rupee-stealing bastard Chintu!

The vendor was too lazy to chase Choti with his legs, so he chased her with his abuses and threats, "*Chal bhag, nahi toh police ko bulaonga!*" Run away or I will call the police to lock you up, Choti heard him shout. She stopped and yelled back: "You greedy, fat-nosed wallah!" she said. "You have so many *ambis*, losing a couple won't make a difference!"

The truth was that the unripe mangoes were not for her, they were for Noor, her beloved friend. This provided a good enough reason for Choti not to feel guilty about taking them, though the vendor's despicable attitude alone made him, at least in her mind, fully deserving of having been relieved of two of his brightest, greenest mangoes.

THE LOST SPRING

Choti ran all the way to the hidden terrace with the heavenly view near her favorite chai-cart, where she had once taken Noor, her heart leaping with anticipation. The two of them had such a pleasant time there before, so peaceful and private and breeze-filled, despite the swarming flies that would, doubtless, join them again. She had so many questions for Noor that it was impossible for Choti to dam up all the questions that spilled from her mouth. She had to learn to be polite, of course, Noor was an elder, and she didn't want to cause her any trouble because she was also a widow.

As Choti ran, she crossed more and more carts piled high with growing mountains of Holi powder: earthen red, rose pink, turmeric yellow, and a dissolvable salt to be mixed with water that was the dark purple of the jamun berry. So many colors soon to be thrown and smeared and cast in the air, or splattered and thrown across many peoples' joyous laughing faces like clouds and explosions from a dream, while wretches like herself groveled for a few rupees, or were starved of any color whatsoever. *All that color going to waste for the pleasure of a chosen few*, Choti thought.

Choti found Noor already sitting on their newfound favorite bench on the terrace. She slowed her steps and snuck up behind her. Then, from behind, Choti thrust one mango and then another in front of Noor's eyes. Noor shivered and put her hand on her heart. Then looked back to see Choti's mischievous grin. "*Uii Ma!* Small one, you scared me more than Lord Yamraja, the God of Death," Noor said. "Suddenly all I could see was a sinful field of green color and it made my heart almost stop."

Choti couldn't keep from laughing.

"Don't do that again!" Noor said. "Or they'll have to take me to Manikarnika sooner than expected. *Uff!* My heart is still beating."

"So sorry, Noor, I only wanted to surprise you."

"You did surprise me, almost to death. Where did you buy the mangoes?" Noor asked, one brow raised, "Hmm?"

"Uh... I... uh... I got them from a fruit-seller I know," Choti said, giggling and looking away to avoid Noor's accusatory eyebrow.

"I see. You *got* them, eh? Don't get thrown in jail, child. You are too young for jail," Noor said.

Choti sat on the bench next to Noor and both started ripping the green skin of the mangoes with their teeth. Soon they were both enjoying the sweet-sour light yellow fruit inside. Noor bit into the fruit and her face lit up like the million lamps of Diwali. Such a taste as she could barely remember, like heaven set upon her palate, but Noor would not express the reality of her pleasure.

Choti spotted Noor's pink book on her lap. "May I take a look?" she said.

"Sure," Noor said, between bites of mango.

Choti reached over and opened Noor's precious book. She flipped through its pages, pin-pointing passage after passage, Tagore's or otherwise, that caught her eye. "What is written here on this page?" Choti inquired, "And this? And this?"

Noor knew every passage and where it was inscribed by heart. The widow's memory was truly impressive. Choti couldn't read, but Noor could recite every passage along with its page perfectly.

Choti cinched up her lips and asked, "Noor, can you teach me to read?"

Noor laughed and ate her last bite of mango. "If you want me to, I will try, I'm not very good at it myself, I recite from memory," Noor said. The emotional bond had already become so strong between them that Noor was willing to undertake such a great task late in life just for Choti. "Now finish your mango. You better eat it before the flies discover it like they did my chai," Noor said, tucking the mango seed into the knot at the end of her saree.

Choti gripped her unripe mango with both hands and started to shamelessly devour it, smacking her lips at its tingling sourness.

"Child, slow down. You'll choke!" Noor said.

"I'm so hungry."

"Enjoy your mango, child, my heart tells me that Anarkali and Chintu will come back to you very soon," Noor said, embracing Choti, her cheeks radiating with a warm glow. "And my heart is rarely mistaken."

Choti looked at Noor and frowned. "I miss them so much and worry about them. With Anarkali on my mind and all the racket the cops make at the gym, I don't even sleep anymore. And, do you know, Raja's potbellied chamchas came to the Sangam Chowk and ordered me not to beg there," Choti blurted all in a rush.

Noor gasped. "How will you survive?"

"I don't know, I will never trust another partner again. I don't want any other partner, now that Chintu cheated me of my money and disappeared," Choti said. Then immediately tried to change the subject: "Noor! Did I ever tell you that Anarkali taught me a begging trick so we would know what our odds were of getting cash from different kinds of people?"

Noor shook her head.

"Anarkali's system is bloody brilliant. For example, someone who is coming back from a relative's cremation at Manikarnika Ghat is almost always more generous," Choti said, and then she stopped to contemplate: "But then, that same someone who gave, say ten rupees, always looks even more sad afterward, it's so strange. They want to give and they don't want to give."

Noor's eyes locked on Choti's. "You only feel the burning body when it's been a part of you. No one else can feel it. That's what makes them more charitable but perhaps also remorseful."

Choti was lingering near Sangam Chowk considering whether or not she should risk begging for rupees from all the cars passing through on their way to or from the ghats—there were so many windows to pound on—when suddenly she was surrounded by people. The mango-vendor had called Inspector Raja's chamchas and now Choti was lost in a forest of potbellies, sticks, and accusatory fingers, the biggest tree being a familiar gourd-like nose.

"This is the girl that stole two mangoes from me and then verbally abused me!" the mango-wallah barked. A big hairy hand clutched Choti's arm and she peeled it off digit-by-digit using her fingernails. "Yeow, don't scratch me," a voice said.

By now the chamchas had raised their sticks and were about to hit her, when out of nowhere, just as Noor had predicted, appeared Anarkali, looking no worse-for-wear. The scene made her livid, and she screamed abuses and threw herself in Choti's defense. Then she grabbed the mango-vendor by the arms and physically shoved him aside. "You don't touch her. If you do, you will seriously regret it," Anarkali said, while Choti darted for cover behind her best friend.

The vendor stared back at Anarkali, fumed and sulked.

"How much for the two mangoes?" Anarkali shrieked. Her sudden looming presence had knocked all of them into silence. "How much for the mangoes, you heartless people!" Anarkali shrieked again.

"One rupee," the vendor said.

Anarkali reached into her blouse and handed the vendor two rupees.

"Now don't ever touch her again," she said.

The vendor grunted as he pocketed his cash and slunk back from wherever he had come. Raja's chamchas were too lazy to do anything else. They just stood around, fondling their sticks and glaring at Choti and Anarkali. "You two aren't out of hot water yet," one of them said. "We're going directly to Inspector Raja to report that you are back and causing trouble again. We'll see what he has to say about it. If I were you, I would never show my face near Sangam Chowk again. Otherwise, it will mean jail…"

"Or worse," said a smaller chamcha, who had puffed his chest so full of his own hot air that his shirt stretched at the buttons.

Then as quickly as they arrived, the gang of chamchas jumped back on their motorbikes, leaving Anarkali with her glaring eyes, and Choti on the verge of tears. Her friend had returned. Choti wrapped her arms around Anarkali's bony waist, which seemed more emaciated than ever.

"I missed you, Anarkali," Choti said, her eyes shining up into Anarkali's bloodshot gaze. "Where did you go? I felt so alone out here."

Now Anarkali's eyes moistened. "I was trying to fly away, little one," she smiled and held Choti's face in her rough hands. "My nightingale, I wanted to fly just like you," she said.

Late at night, in her room at the ashram, Noor stitched a piece of discarded pink rose-patterned cloth into a new frock for Choti. Even lightly holding the colorful cloth burned Noor's hands and eyes, like some deadly contact that beguiled with its beauty. Through squinting eyes in the dim light of the Varanasi moon, Noor measured out a pocket and then went to work on the frock's neck. Her exertion through her shame made it more and more difficult to pass the thread through her needle, and her hands were starting to quiver. She heard Asha's approaching footsteps and hid the frock, still stuck with the needle and strewn with thread, under her thin pillow, making sure that not one inch of frock would bait Asha's probing eyes.

THE LOST SPRING

The next morning Choti expertly shimmied down from her sky-nest and rushed again to the secret terrace off Tulsi Ghat to meet Noor at their bench. In a way, it was like they had never left each other and were simply continuing the conversation they had started.

Noor looked around to make sure no one was standing close enough to hear her speak, and motioned for Choti to crouch closer to her on the bench so she could continue the story she had started:

"So, as I was telling you, Dwarka, the Krishna devotee who had renamed his granddaughter for light, was an ardent believer in freedom," Noor began, then lowered her voice. "Even freedom for women."

Noor's words regarding "freedom for women"—and that included girls—fascinated Choti, completely mesmerizing her.

"To Dwarka, believing in something did not mean the same thing as *acting* on those beliefs. He had actually married off his deceased daughter when she was only 10 years old, a girl who wasn't even capable of birthing a child yet. He blamed this decision on the pressure and superstition of society. It was that sudden shining presence of his new Krishna-blessed granddaughter in his arms that made him feel different. From seeing that first ray of light come to her face and onward, Dwarka believed in acting on his revolutionary but sinful beliefs, and he would dedicate all of them to his light-filled granddaughter, Noor."

Choti gasped softly and touched a finger to her lips, as old widow Noor continued:

"One day Noor began to cry because she was hungry. Dwarka had no idea what to do, so he called out for his wife, Paro, who didn't respond, even as his granddaughter's crying split his ears. When Dwarka walked into their bedroom to see what was going on, he found his wife stewing with anger, looking like she had just lost a war and returned injured from a battlefield. 'Paro! What are you doing in here? Our granddaughter needs you, she won't stop crying,' Dwarka pleaded.

"'So let her cry! Let your precious granddaughter die, in fact. She is Satan's child! The birth of this little evil one is what killed my daughter. And now her own father doesn't want the child. Can we blame him? She killed his wife! Go drown her in the Ganga, don't bring her to me,' Dwarka's wife shrieked.

"His wife's harsh words shook Dwarka to the soles of his feet. But no matter, because Dwarka was already completely dedicated to his little one and couldn't take his eyes off her tiny fingers and fists, her cries of sorrow or hunger or delight, and, especially, the light that seemed to emanate from her.

"After his wife's rejection of her, whenever his granddaughter cried, whether half-asleep in a dream, or half-awake in a nightmare, Dwarka would prepare her feed. He began to dedicate every hour of every day to her. In the mornings, he took her to witness the union of sunrise and Ganga, and though she might have been too young to understand, Dwarka always whispered in Noor's ear to explain that the sun didn't mind living in darkness for a while, because he knew that he would be welcomed by

Ganga the next day. Dwarka also took her to every ghat on the Ganga to witness various ceremonies, and even to secret meetings where revolutionaries discussed how to overthrow the British rulers. They did all their favorite things together, usually accompanied by the eating of the sweetest treats.

"Dwarka celebrated his granddaughter's first steps, her first falls, her laughter, every wave or squeeze of her hands, and her first words, which is what meant most to him, because while most children's first word was 'Ma,' his granddaughter's first word was 'Pa,' and hearing her say it the first time almost broke his heart.

"Some of Dwarka's more conservative friends shared their concern for the name he had given his granddaughter because they thought it sounded Muslim, whereas they were all Hindus, to which Dwarka would cleverly answer, 'Light has no religion, religion is the realm of darkness.' This belief usually left these friends of his aghast."

Choti chimed in, "I agree with Dwarka."

"I believe you," Noor said as she continued: "Noor's light grew brighter as she matured and she became an ever more accurate reflection of Dwarka. Together, Grandfather Dwarka and Granddaughter Noor shared a great life, sharing everything from laughter, bad jokes, philosophical discussions, long walks under the sun, all the pains and pleasures, blessings and secrets of the Ganga, and smaller, but best of all green mango *chaat*—well, Noor never shared her chaat because it was her absolute favorite, with its slices of sour green mango covered in chilli powder, lemon, and salt. Noor's favorite delight always gave her a sore throat and made her cough but how could Dwarka deny his granddaughter what she loved best?"

"One day I too will eat mango chaat," Choti said, "but I'll have mine with less chilli powder."

"Of course, you will," Noor replied.

"One day we will have mango chaat *and* samosas *and* aloo cutlets *and* jalebis *and* chai with lots of sugar, just you and I, and we won't share with anyone, okay Noor?"

Noor laughed, "Okay." And resumed her story:

"One day Dwarka's wife Paro surprised him by starting her day not with a 'good morning' but with a howling and beating of her chest...."

"Why?" Choti said.

"I'll tell you. You see, Janamashtmi had come around again, the day Paro and had Dwarka's only daughter had died giving birth to Noor. Paro was still embittered and heartbroken. That day was also the seven-year anniversary of Dwarka's little light being reborn. He had bought fried breads and sweets so that he and his little Noor could distribute them to all the saints and sages they would meet on the ghats along Ganga. As they were passing out their gifts to everyone, the two grew tired and sat somewhere along the ghats. That's when Noor surprised him with a most difficult question, one Dwarka feared she would one day ask, ever since she had learned to call him Pa—

"'Why doesn't Grandma talk to me?' His little light's questions didn't end there. 'Why is Grandma so angry at me that she shuts the door on me when I want to see her?' Dwarka's little light persisted.

"Dwarka hung his head and stared out over Ganga, then swung his chin back to Noor: 'My light, don't be fooled. The problem is Grandma loves you too much and has no idea how to express it,' Dwarka fibbed, and put his arm around his granddaughter to soothe her. Noor barely nodded.

"It was then that Dwarka reached into his pocket and pulled out a book the color of a lotus flower, which opened with the lines, *'Death is not extinguishing the light; it is only putting out the lamp because the dawn has come.'* The lines were written by Rabindranath Tagore, but rewritten in Dwarka's handwriting.

"From that day on, Dwarka would read to her every day for the next two years, until the day Noor went to her Grandfather's room to wake him up, but couldn't. The keeper of her light had died, and she remembered how some people had arrived to take away his body on a green bamboo bier, as well as how her grandmother beat her own chest again in her room, crying: 'You unlucky girl, first you killed my daughter, now you killed my husband!'

"A few months later, after her morning routine of watching Ganga welcome the sun with its shades of pink or orange or red or other, almost indescribable colors, Noor arrived home and noticed her grandmother's behavior had changed. Paro gave her some nice clothes to wear and gave her a glass of milk to drink. Her grandmother's kind behaviors only filled Noor's heart with suspicion. Something was wrong.

"Before she knew it, Dwarka's innocent little light was draped in a saree of glittering gold that swirled around her, and someone braided her long hair and decorated it with flowers. An hour or so later, she saw her grandmother welcoming a small group of people, including more distant family members with a *pooja thali*, a plate laid out with rice, marigolds, red thread and a smudge of vermilion. Then a priest walked in carrying all the necessary items for a wedding in his bag, and began to draw a few lines on the ground, placing the *havan kund*, the container for the sacrificial fire, in the middle. Before Noor even realized what was going on, she was walking around the fire with the elderly man who was to become, of all things, her husband."

Choti reared back, trying to catch her breath, as Noor now struggled to speak. "Was he a hundred years old?"

"Older," Noor laughed

"Was there a lot of *mithai* at the wedding?" Choti wanted to know about the sweets served to the guests.

"I don't know. Noor was too sick to eat that day. Her elderly groom died a few months later, but Noor did not cry. In fact, she was happy! She felt free. Maybe now she could go back home to her old house, the place that retained her memories of her grandfather, as well as be allowed to visit the ghats at sunrise again. She was filled with hope—until she saw some saints and women dressed in white sarees arrive."

"What did they do?" Choti asked in fear.

"They grabbed her and shaved her head!"

"Sons of pigs! How dare they! If I'd been there, I'd have hit them so hard…" Choti exclaimed.

"Child," Noor said, "from that day on, Dwarka's granddaughter was forced to wear a white saree and sent off to live in an ashram for the rest of her life. She was not allowed to possess anything—no resources, no friendships, no taste, no life or soul, and no color."

"Thank god you still had your grandfather's diary. If he was alive he would have saved you…"

"No dear, he couldn't have. This is the accursed custom of our land."

"What was your husband's name?" Choti said.

Noor smiled wryly. "That's the best part of the story. To this very moment that I'm sitting next to you, I don't know his name! Once I was termed a widow, there were shackles everywhere, I couldn't shake them off, or fight, or even hope to express my opinion against the system," Noor said.

"What are shackles?" Choti said.

"Like the handcuffs they put on thieves."

"But you didn't steal anything! It was they who stole from you! That's so unfair! If I was there I would have given your grandmother a solid thwack!" Choti said loyally.

Noor smiled at her brave little friend and placed one hand on top of the other on her lap. "But your life will be different," she said. "My heart tells me your life will be like one of those birds set free to fly away over the Ganga. In the end, in order to see you, the world will have to look up, not stamp on you with their feet, not make you beg them for rupees."

"How do you know?" Choti said, stiffening her posture again.

Noor tapped the middle of her chest, and Choti nodded. "It's never wrong," Choti said, so delighted that she clapped her hands together and stuck her tongue between her teeth and laughed until her grin seemed glued on her face forever.

"But it might help you fly if you went to school someday," Noor said.

"Hmm, maybe. Chintu used to say the same thing to me. He was trying to collect money to send me to school but then, when we ran short, he tried to gamble and lost everything. You know, when I haven't been on my rope for a while, I dream that I am on it. And then I dream I start bouncing on it until I can fly, and then I see everything in Varanasi from above, and it all looks so small. Sometimes I feel like I can fly, and sometimes I feel like I never will, but wish that I could. It's my dream, to fly. The more Anarkali tells me that I can, and the more you tell me that I can, well, somehow, someday I'm sure that I will. How can grown-ups be wrong, right?" Choti said.

"Child, you are too smart for your own good," Noor said, reaching around to pack up her pink book, her pot of Ganga water, and the memories she had shared, so she could return to her daily routines at the ashram. "I better get back to my tulsi."

As Noor slowly stood and made her way across the terrace, Choti whistled. "Noor!" she said.

Noor stopped and turned around. "Yes?"

"This year, I promise, you and I will play Holi like you and Dwarka did once, and no one—no bloody one—will stop us."

Choti brazenly defied Raja's chamchas' orders to stay away from Sangam Chowk—in fact she happily skipped all the way there from the terrace in her blue slippers, which were starting to fade even more into the vague colors of a midday cloud.

She didn't want to think about what had happened to Anarkali at the hands of Raja, she was just excited to have her back. She was hoping fervently that when she reached Sangam, Anarkali would already be there, her usual sometimes-charming, sometimes-surly self.

Her hope was realized because when she arrived, Anarkali was working the street—dressed in her red Banarsi saree with its bodacious giant gold paisleys—and with more vitriol than ever, pounding on, screaming at, flirting with, blessing, or cursing the occupants of every vehicle that approached from either direction—like Shiva come to earth.

I am so happy that Anarkali is getting into arguments with everyone because I am also getting sick and tired of the system, Choti thought, skipping even faster until she reached her friend, who immediately turned to her. "Hey, Choti!" Anarkali said, fixing one eye on her and the other on all the traffic. "I noticed that Ram Halwai Sweets closed down."

"Yes, Ram Halwai died and his sons had a big fight over his shop," Choti said, feeling important with the news. "I saw it with my own eyes. The son, who looks just like his father, fell on the ground crying like a big baby."

"Do you think he took his red money-box with him?" Anarkali said. "Or his tap?"

Anarkali and Choti both laughed hysterically at this joke, grabbing their aching, unfed bellies.

The sun was reaching its peak, so Choti moved out of the traffic and sat in the shade on the sidewalk to cool off, pushing the toes of her slippers together as if her toes wanted to grapple with one another.

"Anarkali. I just met my widow friend Noor, and she says that I should be educated, because she believes that if I was, then someday I would really be able to fly," Choti said. "Do you agree?"

Anarkali stopped screaming at everyone and everything to cast her eyes up and down Choti. "What I agree with, Choti, is that you should stay away from that old widow," she said.

"Why? She's very kind to me and we're becoming friends."

Anarkali huffed as she approached a car window yelling, gesturing, begging, and flirting.

"I invited her to play Holi with me!" Choti said.

At this Anarkali gasped and stopped her aggressive solicitations to turn her scornful glare at Choti. "Invited a *widow* to play Holi with you? Is your head okay?" Anarkali said.

Several cars drove past. A rickshaw nearly collided with her as Choti confidently nodded.

"Have you gone mad? You know you can't play Holi with a widow," Anarkali said, before turning back to her business, adopting her exaggerated pose and banging on a car window.

"Don't be jealous!" Choti retaliated.

Anarkali turned around slowly, placed one bony hand on her bony hips and pointed a bony finger in Choti's direction. "I'm not jealous," she said.

Choti retreated to relax in the shade at the side of the Chowk, intertwining her fingers behind her head and propping it up. "Okay, okay. Look, Anarkali, that old widow has had a hard life. She also keeps this secret little pink book filled with Tagore quotes her grandfather had written in it and she has memorized. Should I recite some of them to you? Maybe hearing some of them will get you in a better mood, so you don't end up killing one of your customers," Choti said, grinning impishly.

"I doubt it!" Anarkali said, thrusting herself back into the traffic to scream and coerce passersby. "At least you finally recognize that Tagore is *not* that '1000-year-old' widow's grandfather. I *told* you they weren't related!"

Choti frowned and closed her eyes, hoping her smile would return if she could manage to recall the free, soaring feeling she used to feel when she walked on her rope.

"And by the way, do you think I have time for poems?" Anarkali yelled at Choti over the traffic's rumbling din. "I'm fighting monsters from every side, if you haven't noticed."

Choti clenched her jaw. Of course, she had noticed, more than Anarkali knew.

Now her friend swung her head toward the Chowk's signal lights to tease a young man behind the wheel of a car stuck in traffic. "*Oye hoye!* Salman Bhai!"—"Bhai" was the way she greeted any man she encountered—"*Hai*, why don't you look over here sometimes?"

Anarkali's outrageously flirtatious exchanges with her potential customers always made Choti's mouth and eyes pop open, and she exploded with laughter. She didn't really need to imagine rope-walking to bring a smile to her face, or to make her giggle until her stomach hurt—she had Anarkali. "*Yaar*, Anarkali. I missed everything about you. Holi is coming soon. Between that and having you back it's going to make this my best day ever," Choti said.

A familiar dreaded figure on a motorcycle zigzagged through traffic, and headed straight for Anarkali. Choti backed away to watch Inspector Raja, his teeth gritted, his eyes red and glaring, one of his hands already holding his stick in a tight fist above his head. The sight of the enraged chief threatening to accost her best friend erased any trace of Choti's happiness and sent a tremor through her body.

"Where did you disappear to?" Raja said, blocking Anarkali's movement with his bike. "How many days can you hope to avoid me and save yourself?" Raja shouted angrily.

Anarkali froze in the middle of the intersection and remained that way even as the signal turned green and unleashed another wave of potential customers, whose potential rupees Raja's appearance had caused her to lose.

Raja belly-laughed, cocked his head, and smiled. "Now what will you do, hijra? Your river of rupees just flowed away downstream—if you don't come to see me tonight, that will be the end of you, clear?"

Anarkali had no words. Raja gripped his stick with both hands and hit Anarkali's healthy arm with it. Anarkali winced and grabbed her elbow as Raja accelerated away, vanishing amidst the thickening traffic of early afternoon.

As soon as Raja was out of view, Choti raced to Anarkali's side and hugged her tight. "I hate that man, and I am very scared of him," Choti said.

Anarkali rubbed her arm. "He's trying to destroy me, bit by bit, limb by limb, but don't be afraid, little sister. It's me he's after."

"I'll do whatever I can to protect you," said Choti.

"I believe you, but promise me you won't be naïve. Remember, you need to fly someday," Anarkali said, and reaching into her saree blouse, pulled out the day's take of rupees. "Take these, you'll need them to buy powder to celebrate Holi."

Choti looked up into Anarkali's eyes, puzzled. "But, you might need the money," she said.

"Maybe not," Anarkali said.

Since she had returned, Anarkali's eyes had gone vacant, as cold and dead as winter, like they had never witnessed the bloom of spring. Never before had Choti seen Anarkali's lively and mischievously angry eyes look so listless and dull, even scared. Something in them signaled a change for the worse.

Anarkali gently removed Choti's arms from around her waist. "I better go," she said. Anarkali headed back into the traffic and weaved blindly through it, without any heed for the accelerating traffic. It was a miracle that no car or rickshaw cut her down.

Choti watched her friend limp through traffic like a wounded animal to the far side of the intersection, and disappear beyond the traffic into a tangle of narrow, intersecting streets. A queasy feeling tugged at Choti's throat and gut, the nausea of thinking she might never see her friend again, though admittedly, Anarkali always seemed to surprise her.

The Faces in the Shadows

Vanished identities clinging to faith

Anarkali took a deliberately round-about route as she hurried through the sun-and-smoke-filled Varanasi air and descended the rickety ladder to her secret underground Temple of Fireflies. She had returned home in an attempt to escape. But she knew the respite would be short-lived. Anarkali knew Raja would punish her severely that night. She winced as she imagined the blows of his stick. That was nothing new. But somehow Anarkali knew it would be a worse beating than ever before, perhaps the worst ever. In a strange, relative way, a way only someone caught in the dance between those in authority and those who have nothing could understand, she fully deserved it. Or did she?

Now entombed in her Temple of Fireflies, Anarkali lay in the dark, flat on her back on her bed of wooden planks, feeling the warming breeze from the sewer stream flowing beneath her bed as it wafted across her weary, half-broken body. The stream's temperature was rising, as it always did when Ganga's spring swell began. Somewhere in the distant mountains, in the far-off land of Ganga's source, the snows were thawing, the ice was cracking, but Anarkali felt anything but warmth. Her heart had turned into a cold stone, incapable of feeling any trace of love or pain.

She shouldn't have blackmailed Raja by threatening to expose him to his wife. But that was not the only reason Anarkali's heart had gone cold.

Anarkali had once stationed herself by the steps leading down to Lolark Kund, raucously blessing every woman who passed by to give birth to a Ram-like son: virtuous, brave, honorable, and obedient—when she saw Raja's wife, Rani, making her descent.

It was on the auspicious day of Lolark Shasthi that everyone in Raja's family, even his own daughters, were excited about Rani's visit to Lolark Kund for a holy dip at the bottom so she might one day, finally, birth a son. Like the other son-eager women, Rani was all decked out in a gold-edged saree with lots of jewelry, wearing colorful glass bangles and flowers in her hair. So decked out was she that Rani positively clinked as she moved, up to the point of becoming lost in the vast cascade of women descending the steps for the same pressured reasons.

Rani neither dipped so much as a toe in the waters, nor left behind any of the ornaments she wore, in Lolark Kund. Well—why would she? Just to satisfy everyone at home? The ornaments might better be used for her daughters' education. Would she toss her newest saree into the well? No. She would leave an old one somewhere on the majestic steps above.

In her heart, Rani knew that Raja, the son of his harsh father, would never be, and never could be, faithful to his professional duties, or to her. Every corrupt rupee that entered their house only added to what was already a national bank of curses; curses marked with the fingerprints of the weak, of the poor and fallen, or those innocent souls who still believed that justice would somehow prevail, even in their silence. In this way, Rani would always be cursed, but she hoped her daughters wouldn't be. Having a son whom she was certain would be just like his father would only curse everyone more.

Would Anarkali bless such a woman to have a son? Absolutely not. Anarkali only glared and said nothing. Rani too noticed how the usually effusive, fortune-telling hijra had suddenly gone mute when she passed by.

It was Rani's sudden frown and down-turned eyes that proved she understood the hijra's reason for withholding her blessing. They both knew that Raja's son would be the devil incarnate. Rani would never bear Raja a son. All this, Anarkali could surmise.

This episode, coupled with the darker ones shared between Anarkali and Inspector Raja, were what made everything so different today. Things had gotten deeply, troublingly personal between them.

As for Raja and Rani, the every-day, every-night tangles and grinding gears of actions and inactions, violence and shame and chivalry, husband and wife found themselves in, would transform into the endless night of nightmare visions that now shook Anarkali to her skinny bones.

The strange triangle they made was all so sordid.

In her snakehole beneath Varanasi, Anarkali's stomach churned with fear and she shivered as though a fever were coming on. It took all her strength to try to detach, stay warm, and keep her eyes open.

When, finally, Anarkali's eyelids did close (seeking death, perhaps?) a small miracle occurred. An internal, deeply sonorous voice told her to open her eyes. She did as the voice commanded, and upon doing so, Anarkali woke not into her rough and sullied life, but into a dream, a dream composed of hundreds of swarming fireflies of every imaginable hue flying—no, dancing!—around in fantastic, ever-shifting shapes and patterns all around her room, like Holi exploding early, and just for her. The swirling, shifting dots and fantastic streaking colors delivered back Anarkali's hope.

Perhaps I will survive to witness Spring, Anarkali thought, as she got up and climbed her rickety bamboo ladder to face her demon.

It was a special day because it was the day Choti, rich with the money Anarkali had given her, had promised to take Noor for samosas at her favorite samosa place in Sangam Chowk. For this special occasion, Choti had stuck a delicate paper flower of faded orange in her hair. Even if Noor would never reveal it, Choti's hope was that the flower would bring the color of joy into Noor's eyes.

The two met at their usual bench, just off the terrace, and walked arm-in-arm to the samosa shop in the Chowk. This samosa shop was the hot-spot that every Ganga-bound pilgrim stopped at for a last quick bite and hot chai before seeking the purifying waters.

Halwai's wasn't really a "shop," it was more an open-air arrangement: a crooked counter around which were strewn a motley collection of weather- and ghat-beaten chairs and tables on the verge of collapse. Nonetheless, in Choti's opinion, the spicy potato samosas served here were Varanasi's best.

Choti led Noor by the hand and saw the proprietor, in his white *banian* vest that was stained and soaked with sweat. Beside him was the *kadhai*, the large wok filled with bubbling hot oil in which the samosas were being deep-fried. The skinny fifty-year-old waiter who worked for him not only suffered the owner's watchful, beady eyes as he prepared and packed orders behind the counter, but also suffered them as he took orders and otherwise attended to the twenty or so seated guests the place could hold.

What was apparent from the skinny waiter's knife-like glances was that the favorite part of his job was taking out his frustrations and anger on his customers. He passed on his boss's treatment of him directly onto his customers. This maltreating service was the waiter's victory, his revenge, his power, his entitlement, his reward for suffering under his superior. In a way, this made the samosa shop experience all the more exclusive and "full-service." For such consistently distasteful service to result in such consistently delicious samosas was nothing short of another Varanasi miracle, one worth every contemptuous look from the proprietor and his waiter.

The proprietor's peripheral vision tracked Choti and Noor as they walked behind the waiter and ignored his frantic shooing-away movements, to a table, if it could be called that, at the farthest corner from him. Their gumption challenged the skinny waiter's authority—as thin and meager as it really was—so much so that rather than greeting them the first thing the skinny waiter did was drop everything he was doing and turn off the fan, a clear signal that he wouldn't be offering service to patrons of such low stature as a street waif and a widow.

The waiter's rude action did nothing to deter Choti. "*Ey! ey!* Waiter! Two samosas and two *kadak*, stiff, chais," she demanded, raising her hand like all the other adult pilgrims around. Noor sat with her head lowered, blushing with shame. She was completely overwhelmed, and sank lower in her chair, with no pride whatsoever, visibly guilty for having the gall to enter the shop in the first place, and especially guilty for being led in by a child.

Choti reached across the table to clutch Noor's hand, but Noor pulled it away.

"Noor," Choti said. "So sorry to put you through this, but these samosas are the *best*. If you feel uncomfortable, you can just stare at the flower in my hair." Choti tilted her head so Noor's eyes would have no chance of missing its orange petals.

Instead of serving her and Noor, the waiter went over and stood near the counter to whisper his complaints into the proprietor's hair-sprouting, flappy ears. The proprietor nodded, deepened his frown, furrowed his brow and glared back at Choti and Noor.

And, so the waiting began. Choti glanced at the waiter and his overlord behind their crooked counter. For twenty minutes now, the halwai had sat idle, staring unblinkingly at Noor and Choti, refusing them service, denying their appetite—and for his *own* samosas—and causing their stomachs to whine and groan. The fan had yet to be turned back on. To Choti, twenty minutes of hunger was twenty minutes too long. She looked at Noor, who had started to sweat.

"Choti," Noor said finally, "I really appreciate what you were trying to do for me but no one's going to serve the likes of us. We better leave."

As they made their way out of the shop, bellies empty, three other guests—Privileged Ones, in Choti's estimation—entered and found a table in the center, an action which sent the waiter tripping over himself, seemingly reincarnated from the grave, to welcome them with a beaming smile. He even turned on the fan and directed its spinning blades at his new guests so they could cool off as he enthusiastically took their order, while also finding the time to inquire if they had come to Varanasi so they could witness the evening aarti soon to transpire nearby.

Choti turned and stuck her tongue out at the waiter: "I even had the money to pay today, and still you denied me; I'll just steal them the next time, you wait and see."

Choti and Noor walked back to the broken sidewalks strewn about the ghats. Their bellies ached with hunger pangs and, for a while, as they walked together, they didn't speak. The more they walked, the more Choti fumed, until she suddenly stamped her foot on the ground.

"I'm so angry at that bloody skeleton of a waiter. All I wanted was to share my favorite samosas with you, and that bloody bastard had to keep me from doing it," Choti said, digging all over herself for something.

"It's fine, child. That's life," Noor said, cracking a forgiving smile.

"That doesn't have to be 'life,' Noor," Choti said. "I wasn't even asking for free samosas! I was happy to pay!"

"Like I always say, that's life," Noor shrugged philosophically.

"Well, if that's life, life's not fair. I've seen so many people sitting and eating samosas here," Choti continued. "They line up to eat them. Once I begged there and someone gave me a piece of samosa, and it was the best thing I ever ate in my life. All I wanted to do today was share that delicious taste with you. Maybe I'm too small and lowly for anyone to take seriously," Choti stamped her foot again. "Ugh!"

Noor shook her head and clicked her tongue. "Choti, child! You're not lowly at all." She pointed to a concrete bench. "Let's rest our famished bodies on that bench."

They reached the bench and sat down next to each other. Noor took a slow, deep breath and glanced down at Choti, who was still fuming and had started to violently kick her legs back and forth to vent her frustration.

"Choti," Noor said. "Do you know what an eclipse is?"

Choti shook her head.

"It's when the much smaller moon blocks out the entire sun and causes the whole world to go dark. One of my fondest memories from when I was young was seeing an eclipse with my grandfather. In that rare miraculous moment, the usually smaller, shyer moon suddenly becomes big and powerful enough to hide the usually more majestic, more powerful sun. And when it does, everyone, I mean *everyone*, both then and now, is awed by its power," Noor said.

"Kind of like me when I'm on my rope, everyone looks up to me when I'm above them, in the sky," Choti said, grinning.

Noor beamed. "I wish you see it sometime. It is like a victory of good over evil, like when Lord Rama defeated the evil Ravana, like a re-writing of the edict of the natural order of things, about who is powerful and who is not. When I witnessed it, and sensed the awe and fear it caused in others, I was filled with hope. I thought, so it is possible for the weak to overcome the strong; it is possible to re-write the rules? Choti, do you understand me, Choti?"

Choti stopped kicking her feet, absolutely mesmerized. "I *think* I do."

"You remind me of that eclipsing moon, my child. One day, you will have the power to change the order of things."

Watching Noor's face grow animated as she spoke, it seemed to Choti like the moon itself. Radiant, wise, gentle, shining a small light to one eclipsed in the dark.

"The moon can be just as powerful as the sun, but it's got a cooler brightness and glows soft, so you can see it without hurting your eyes. There is more truth to the moon for that reason. And it's so powerful it can even pull water from the rivers and seas and send it across the earth. If Choti is small, then she is small like the moon, which is not small at all."

Climbing back into her sky-nest after seeing off Noor, Choti was sure she had been spotted by one of Raja's goons. This would be very bad. Choti prayed fervently to Ganga Ma. She prayed that she was wrong and no one had seen her sneak in. She lay down on her back and hoped to fall asleep, when a skinny black cat passed by, meowing and then lulling itself into a purr at her shoulder. She shooed it away because it seemed like bad luck, the last kind of luck she needed.

 Choti closed her eyes and covered her ears, but still heard the growl of motors and saw the beam of headlights. Raja's swarm of motorcycle-riding potbellies had arrived back at the gym. She heard them collect at their usual spot near their sandbox of weights. There was something even more reckless and dangerous about their grunting and laughing that day. She thought of the savage ferocity with which they had ravaged her teddy bear and ripped it to shreds.

 What she heard next, she had heard before in the same circumstances, but this time it froze her.

 It was Anarkali's voice.

 She was screaming in pain!

Choti huddled further in fright but couldn't shut out the thrashing and screams that echoed off the concrete walls of the gym. She heard Anarkali beg the beasts to forgive her for not cooperating with them. When she heard Anarkali shout her name—something about excusing her for her petty crimes—she uncovered her ears, opened her eyes, and looked through the peephole to see what was really going on. Immediately, she wished she hadn't.

Bloody Raja appeared out of the shadows and went straight for Anarkali's throat. Choti wanted to jump down and attack them with everything she had, which, compared to them, wasn't much. Raja was hitting Anarkali with his stick. The animals were making too many drunken sounds to understand what they were saying. Some of the chamchas were even laughing at what was going on. Choti slipped on her cardboard floor and it made a dull thud. Everyone stopped what they were doing, except Anarkali who had fallen to her knees and looked like she was about to faint. She looked so meek, not at all like the devil-may-care beggar who dared force to a stop any vehicle in the traffic at Sangam Chowk.

Choti prayed that no one thought the noise came from her. Luckily, the cat slipped out and ran across the gym.

Raja towered over Anarkali "So, you bloody hijra, you said you will tell my wife about me? About *me*? You exist only on my leftovers, you understand? You only exist because I *allow* you to exist," Raja said, and punched Anarkali in the face. Choti felt like she had been punched in the face too, but she didn't cry.

Anarkali fell to the side, groaning and writhing in pain while Raja's chamchas started tearing off her clothes. Animals! Bastards! Half of her clothes were off, she was almost naked. Her sister! Anarkali tried to crawl away. Choti was ashamed that she was too scared to help.

Then the shadows, Raja's obedient drunken horde of cops, moved in and held a naked Anarkali in place until she stopped screaming. Raja then calmly pulled out his gun and pulled the trigger. There was a resounding bang and Anarkali slumped to the ground.

Am I dead, too? Choti thought, she couldn't feel anything anymore. It was the numb feeling of weightlessness, the numb feeling of death. A dead person cannot move, so she *must* have died. Even Raja's drunk and boisterous chamchas seemed to have died, no longer making any sound. The gun went off again, and this time Choti counted its echoes—one off the gym walls, another off Sangam Chowk, another off Tulsi Ghat, another off the Nameless House with Pink Walls, the final one off Manikarnika, where those lucky enough had already been turned to ash.

No one moved.

Choti felt that all the witnesses to that moment of Anarkali's death were acutely aware of each other's presence, like they were trapped in some silent theatrical performance.

"Throw this bastard hijra's sin-filled body into the Ganga," Raja's command broke the sudden stillness of the night.

Choti felt smaller and more insignificant than she ever had before.

The next morning a weak morning sun awakened Choti's deadened body. She must have been crying through the nightmares she had because her eyes were swollen and encrusted. Luckily, she had been smart enough to insert a swatch of saree into her mouth to muffle any sounds of inadvertent screams and stop her teeth from chattering.

That day Choti was more determined than ever to beg at Sangam Chowk, all by herself, in Anarkali's memory. In a way, and with her friend's blessing—or perhaps, her curse—the Chowk had become as much her turf as it had been Anarkali's. In the past, when one of them hadn't been there in flesh and blood, they had been there in spirit and grace. And from the previous night and every day onward, all that remained of Anarkali for Choti to rely on was that spirit and grace. She was too young to admit it to herself, but Noor's words, *that's life*, kept drilling at her brain as she started to work the traffic again, now sans her best friend.

As she looked around with listless eyes Choti noticed that Ram Halwai Sweets was gone and a new owner was ensconced in his place with a sign that read, "Basant Sweets," already affixed in preparation for the coming of Holi.

Suddenly, as Choti approached a line of cars, Raja revved-up alongside her on his motorbike, looking beaten and old, as if now death had been chasing and running him ragged. Raja could barely hold Choti's gaze as he suspiciously probed her eyes. Every twitch of Raja's tired eyes sent a tremor through Choti.

Choti did not blink when Inspector Raja suddenly reached out and grabbed her by the hair. "So, your name is Choti," Raja said. Every motorist, every person walking by, was stunned to see the big hefty cop yanking the hair of a small street girl, but no one intervened.

"Where does Anarkali live?" Raja said, obsessively looking around and fidgeting with his mustache. Perhaps she had hidden some evidence there that incriminated the cop and he wanted to destroy.

The question shocked Choti to the soles of her feet, but she kept her expression as straight as she had once held her balancing stick. "How would I know?" Choti said, shrugging. "I've never gone to her house. All I know is that she didn't show up today." Choti's eyes chose the swelling traffic over Raja's sallow eyes. She would not grant her friend's murderer even one accidental blink of respect.

Raja released Choti's hair. "I don't want to see you in this area again, you can't beg here anymore, this is my area," Raja the murderer said. "I was doing your friend Anarkali a favor allowing her to beg here."

Choti refused to meet his eye.

"Understand, girl? Now get out of here! If I ever see you here again, I will do much worse things to you than pull at your hair," Raja said, his voice quivering with rage as he looked around threateningly before gunning his bike and speeding off toward his preferred cigarette kiosk.

A sudden downpour drenched the next few hours with torrential rain. Choti, wet and still numb from her encounter with Raja, walked onto the hidden terrace near Tulsi Ghat, where she had fixed to meet Noor.

Noor had been waiting a long time for her, and when Choti saw her friend sitting on their bench waiting for her, staring into the parting, sun-releasing clouds, Choti stumbled over to fall into Noor's lap, shivering and weeping.

At first, Noor resisted the urge to comfort and hug her friend in public but then she let her arms cover and embrace her distraught young friend. Choti's little body shook with sobs and her unstopping tears dampened Noor's saree.

"Noor, Anarkali's dead, the bloody animals killed her. I saw it with my own eyes. Raja shot and killed her," Choti wept, not even bothering to lift her face as she wiped off her nose and mouth with her hand.

Noor's face became instantly alert. Her eyes sharpened. "Ram, Ram, Ram. May Satan fall on all of them. This Raja is a Ravana, a real devil."

Noor hugged Choti, then kneeled down beside her, deep lines of concern forming on her face. Now Noor trembled, too.

"You saw them?" asked Noor urgently, "But did anyone see you?"

Choti's chest started to heave. "No, as much as I wanted to, I couldn't utter a word or make any sound. I was so scared, Noor, I couldn't help my friend. Bloody bastards. I hate Raja. One day, when I become big enough, I will give him the karma he deserves, I swear."

Noor rubbed Choti's back and holding her in her lap rocked Choti back and forth trying to soothe her. An hour or so later, Choti finally lifted her face. Her eyes were swollen, and she had gone as pale as if she herself had died.

"Poor, poor child," Noor said. "Let me show you something. Maybe it will lift your mood." Noor pulled out the frock she had hand-stitched for her. It was covered in huge, brightly colored flowers and, best of all, it had a big front pocket where Choti could keep all of the rupees she would earn in the future.

Choti had no words, but managed a wan smile as she took the frock in her hands. It was absolutely beautiful. "I don't know what to say," Choti said.

"You've lost your best friend, you needn't say anything," said Noor.

"This frock is too beautiful. I don't deserve it," Choti said and began to cry again. "I'm not worthy of it, Noor, I just lost a friend and didn't do anything to help her. I'm worthless, I don't deserve it."

"Quiet your mouth, child, don't be silly," Noor said. "I made it just for you. It's only a frock, a piece of material I threw together, but I hope someday by wearing it you will be happy again."

"Thank you," Choti said, and leaned her weary head on Noor's thin, white-draped shoulder.

"You are welcome, Choti. Now run and change into your frock behind the temple, near Lolark Kund. If you stay in these wet clothes, you'll catch a fever."

Choti got up and walked towards the temple, clutching her new flower-covered dress, which made her feel like some lovely garden in motion. It would be the first time in her life she would wear new clothes.

A few days later, a visibly subdued Choti, in her new frock, was back, sitting quietly next to Noor on their terrace bench, observing the pilgrims and aarti and Holi visitors in the distance amid the ghats. Suddenly a stranger, a tall woman dressed in a starched saree, and bell-shaped gold earrings approached her.

Choti's eyes flared in fear as the tall woman came closer and bent her knees to look Choti straight in the face. "Such a lovely dress," the woman said in a kind voice.

Choti looked away.

Then the woman continued: "I'm a reporter from the *India Crime* newspaper in New Delhi. My name is Rekha, Rekha Saxena. Didn't you and a person who went by the name 'Anarkali' beg together on Sangam Chowk?" the woman asked.

Choti began to tremble in fear.

Noor immediately put her arm around her friend. "Why do you want to know?" she demanded.

"Choti…" Rekha the reporter started to say something.

Immediately Choti thrust out her chin and stiffened her shoulders, now on guard. "How do you know my name?"

"I can explain later, but don't worry, I'm on your side. I care about what happened to Anarkali," said Rekha. "I heard about her body being found, and I'm investigating her death."

"I wish I could help you, but I only worked for Anarkali. I don't know what happened to her, we weren't really friends," Choti lied, too scared to get involved.

Noor looked at Rekha sternly: "We don't know anything about Anarkali. Now stop bothering the child."

Rekha courteously nodded to the old widow, but then turned back to Choti. "You do know your friend Anarkali was murdered, right?" she said.

"No, I didn't. I don't know anything. She was a good boss and seemed like a nice person," Choti pretended not to know anything. "I am really sorry to hear that."

"Do you have any idea who might have murdered her?" Rekha said. "Like someone she had dealings with, or owed something to, anything like that you can remember?"

Noor had to intervene, and raised her voice. "Reporter Rekha, this is a child you are asking all these questions. She doesn't know anything, can't you see? Why are you trying to drag her into this mess?"

"I'm sorry. May I know your name?" Rekha said.

"My name is Noor. Now please leave this poor child alone."

"But we want to bring the murderer to justi—"

"—You can? You promise? Then I know who killed Anarkali," Choti said suddenly, cutting Rekha off and prompting Noor to exclaim, "Child! Stay out of it, you've been through enough in life."

Choti turned to Noor. "I know, Noor, but Anarkali was my best friend and someone has to punish these bloody animals. Don't worry about me," Choti said, and turned back to Rekha.

Rekha had already grabbed Choti's hand and was now leading the girl toward the edge of the terrace and back into the streets.

Noor shook her head, then closed her eyes in silent prayer.

Rekha marched into the Nagar Nigam police station holding Choti by the hand with the intention of filing an

F.I.R., the First Information Report for the criminal offence of the murder of Anarkali.

The Nagar Nigam sat high on Ganga's banks and was the main Varanasi police headquarters from where Raja, the King, lorded over everyone, and, at least in his mind, perhaps lorded over even Ganga herself.

As they entered, Choti saw all the goons she had witnessed from her sky-nest a week before at the police gym, now glaring at her from their tea-swilling huddle.

Choti's first instinct was to flee, but her second instinct was a feeling that if she did flee, it would make her appear guilty of whatever the chamchas wanted to make her appear guilty of. Her third and fourth more terrifying instincts were that someone on that terrible night had not been fooled by the cat, or that someone on the Chowk had told Raja where she slept at night, and therefore must have witnessed any violent actions that had occurred at the gym, past or present, including Anarkali's murder.

Rekha leaned down to whisper in Choti's ear while holding her hand: "Choti, I don't know what you know or don't know. The point is that we must punish these corrupt bastards for what they have done to Anarkali, and probably to many others like her, and probably to children like you. Even if they hold the keys of power, we have the right to open the doors to what is right."

Rekha straightened up and together they walked to the front desk. "Officer," she demanded. "I want to file an F.I.R. over the murder of Anarkali."

The officer behind the desk put down his tea and leaned his elbows on its filthy, samosa-crumbs and chai-stained surface, as Rekha went on: "She was killed last week at your very own gymnasium and then her body was dumped in the Ganga and was discovered near Sangam, where the locals identified it. It was sent for a post-mortem. And the doctor's verdict is homicide. The bullet has been identified. Now we have a witness."

"Is this street urchin your key witness?" the officer said, wiping off his mouth with studied casualness as he looked down at Choti. "This girl you've brought with you is just trying to make a quick buck by manipulating you out of your money, so you can report some fake news story. We see kids like her all the time. She's not to be trusted; we know her, she's already been caught and warned for stealing. I can only imagine what other crimes she's committed, especially if she was hanging around with that criminal, Anarkali."

Choti was struck numb with fear as those who were supposed to protect and serve revealed themselves to possess the most evil faces of society she had ever come across.

Another, even brawnier police officer, a known tyrant to street children with a particularly nasty reputation among them for extreme cruelty and corruption, approached the desk.

He checked out Rekha from top to bottom but focused his vitriol on Choti, allowing his eyes to shamelessly bore into hers: "So is this your witness?" he said, cracking his knuckles.

Choti had seen this goon at the gym that night too; he was always hanging around with Raja and was one of his main lackeys.

"Officer, don't dare try to intimidate this helpless girl," Rekha said, pointing her finger in the officer's face. The reporter pulled out her I.D. "These poor people you lord over may be invisible, but I'm certainly not."

Suddenly, there was an explosion of people as every officer swarmed in to check Rekha's credentials. Now she had everyone's attention. Choti had never seen such power wielded by a woman before, and she had the strangest, most alien feeling: the feeling of safety.

"Now who's in charge here?" Rekha said.

Whether it was planned or not, Rekha had managed to get all Raja's chamchas together in the room. "Choti, don't be afraid. Take a good look around. You saw what happened. Do you recognize any of these people? Anyone who was involved in what happened to your friend?"

Choti bravely stepped back and away from her new protector. If her widening eyes were any indication, she would have had to say, *all of them*. But fear struck and Choti said nothing, just stood looking in incensed disbelief at the line of bloodthirsty animals in uniforms.

"Choti, don't be afraid to speak out, the law is here to protect you, and I will certainly see that it does," said Rekha.

It was at this point that Inspector Raja swaggered into his station—a strutting, leering entrance that sent Choti hiding for cover behind Rekha's blue saree.

Raja surveyed the scene, waving his baton, puffing out his chest and placing one fist on his hips, his potbelly bulging like it always did: "What is this tamasha going on?" Raja thundered.

Rekha had her murderer, she was certain of it, just by looking at him. She was more certain when Choti reached around and almost squeezed off the fingers of her hand. And then there was no more uncertainty when Choti said, "They were *all* there and it was Raja who fired the gun!"

Rekha observed Raja's reaction closely. He had certainly been rattled by what Choti had to say.

"Inspector, my apologies for letting this, as your colleague so poetically put it, 'untrustworthy and manipulative,' little girl run her mouth off," Rekha said. Then she turned to the station superior again. "Officer, if you refuse to file a report against Inspector Raja and his underlings, I am heading straight to the Delhi High Court to ensure that you will never lay eyes on your Varanasi home again. I will ensure full rights for the deceased Anarkali, as well as this girl."

Rekha's confident words sent all the officers into hiding as the station officer reluctantly pulled out his ledger and finally took down the F.I.R. as Rekha dictated.

Rekha and Choti stepped out of the police station onto the street. They both took a deep breath, as if they had just survived an earthquake.

Choti tugged at the edge of Rekha's saree. "Lady, is Anarkali really gone?"

Rekha bent down before the little girl to break the news as gently as she could: "Choti, I am sorry to say, yes, what you saw really happened. It wasn't a dream. Anarkali was murdered and she is dead. I know this because her body was found where Ganga meets the Sangam Chowk. It washed up on the banks there," Rekha said, closing her eyes.

Was this woman, a perfect stranger, saying a prayer for her friend, someone she never knew? Choti thought. That Anarkali's body had washed up in the same spot where the two of them had spent so much time together wasn't in itself good news, but this random return to where their friendship started seemed to indicate something.

Choti glanced back at the police station—a healthy survival instinct she had learned from Anarkali—and saw Raja braced in the doorway, with his glinting eyes, and his demented, evil grin still stuck on his face even after the terrible thing he had done. Now Raja's leering presence did not make Choti cower, it made her want to vomit.

Rekha placed her arm around Choti's shoulders and led her away. She hailed a rickshaw and helped Choti climb in. "Don't worry, we will punish all of these culprits, as soon as I get back to New Delhi," Rekha said as they rode along. "Then the wheels of justice will finally turn." Choti did not respond, just stared numbly down the road.

On her way back to her sky-home, Choti saw a sadhu, a saffron-robed ascetic with sandalwood paste smeared on his forehead, and a fortune-telling parrot. The sadhu squatted on the roadside talking to a patron, a man who no doubt wanted to know what his future held for him.

The parrot picked a card from several that lay in front of him, face down on a mat. As she and Rekha passed closer by in their rickshaw, Choti cocked her head to listen as the sadhu read the card the parrot had picked. *"You can escape the City of Death, but not Death itself,"* he said. Even parrots knew the truth. Choti suddenly felt very dizzy, dizzy enough that she thought she might be on the verge of her own early death.

Rekha ordered the rickshaw-puller to stop. They had come to the path that led to the terrace where they had first met. Rekha had promised to deliver Choti back to where she had found her, at Noor's side. Choti turned to Rekha and gave her a quick shy hug, then jumped off the rickshaw without looking back. When she went onto the hidden terrace, Noor was nowhere to be seen. An alarmed Choti went searching for her near the bench and looked down towards Ma Ganga. There she was, holding her brass pot and her Tagore book, waiting for Choti on the ghat below.

For that moment, Choti felt relieved. For that moment, all was well.

A Pouch of Color

Borrowed hope,
rented courage, stolen color

Noor walked back to the terrace bench with her brass pot, which was now full of Ganga water, and sat down next to Choti, who had been patiently waiting for her. Choti's patience was not normal, for it was a sullen patience. If anything, she probably retained more leg-kicking yearning than the average child, but the patience she experienced that day on the bench was more like helplessness, a feeling she rarely felt. Then again, how could she not feel helpless, or know whom to trust, with Anarkali gone?

Noor sat with her brass pot on her lap. Choti inhaled and wrinkled her nose. "Ganga is in a bad mood today," she said.

"Why do you say that, child?" Noor said.

"They found Anarkali, or what was left of her body, washed up on Ganga's banks," Choti said.

Noor gasped and set her pot on the ground. Her eyes grew large with compassion and concern.

"They killed Anarkali, and now I'm sure they are going to kill me, squash me like some little mosquito. I told you I was too small," Choti said, laying her head in Noor's lap. She could smell the Ganga in her white saree.

Noor bent down to gather Choti in an embrace. "Oh no. That is the worst news I've ever heard. I'm so sorry."

Choti sniffled and Noor felt patches of moisture on her lap. "Can you feel my heart, child?"

Choti closed her eyes and nodded. "Yes, even through your legs," she said.

"Everything will be okay," Noor said, and started to run her fingers through Choti's hair. "Oh! Look there is already some good news," Noor said as her fingers stroked the child's head.

Choti's eyes slowly opened. "What is it?"

"The good news is that I don't see any more lice in your hair, the oil I gave you before seems to have worked!"

Choti's lips released her teeth, but as quickly as they did, her lips recaptured them. How could she let herself smile at a time like this?

"Noor," Choti said, "It was Raja and his chamchas who killed Anarkali. I saw them beat her, torture her, hunt her down and shoot her. It was Raja who pulled the trigger."

Noor gasped and hugged her tighter. "My God, unbelievable, the evil of mankind," Noor said.

"And then Raja and his chamchas carried Anarkali's body off and tossed it into Ganga like a piece of trash," Choti said, and buried her face once again in Noor's lap. "These guys are worse Ravanas than the one in the *Ramayana*. They will not leave me alone now. I'm sure they already have their eyes on me. I have no idea what to do, or where to go," Choti said.

"Child, my poor child," Noor said, starting to rub Choti's back.

"Noor, you told me I was big, you told me to stand up so I could fly. That's the right thing to do, and I know it, and you taught me this. I didn't fly when they murdered Anarkali, yet I watched the whole thing. Was I right or wrong? I was too scared, but was that selfish? I don't know what's right and wrong anymore. And the world doesn't seem to care either way," Choti said.

"You were not right or wrong, you were just scared. But even though you were scared, you are still braver than most," Noor replied. She gently turned Choti's head by the chin until she could see the girl's eyes. "You know who is scared?"

"Who?" said Choti.

"Raja and his chamchas. What the murderers are really scared of is the truth coming out, which means that underneath their ugly skin they are scared of you. You know the truth and they know that you know it. There might be many of them, but my heart tells me the whole Universe is with you, just as I am," Noor said. Then she asked, "What is this lady from Delhi's name again?"

"Rekha. She is a journalist from *India Crime* newspaper. She says that I am doing the right thing by getting involved. I even told Raja in front of all his boys at the station that he was the one who murdered Anarkali! You should have seen the look on his face," Choti said. "Now I'm so scared they will find a way to kill me. I know if they had their way they would burn me like a piece of wood. All I have in life now is myself, and you. I don't want to die. I still want to fly above everyone's heads one day," Choti said.

All this while Rekha had been keeping a watch over them, at a distance behind the bench, sipping her chai. Looking around her, she marveled at how the growing mounds of red, green, yellow, purple, blue color, and the growing mounds of mithai, the addictively sweet treats from Varanasi, were steadily transforming every cart, stall, kiosk and market, in readiness for Holi. Color seemed to have overtaken everything. Rekha was being blinded by color, but then Rekha's eyes saw only in black-and-white—for a gang of Raja's goons, the same sullen faces she and Choti had confronted at the police station, was charging down a crowded market alley and headed for the terrace.

Rekha ran to the bench where Noor and Choti sat. "Sorry to disturb you, but we have to leave. Choti's not safe here!" she said urgently.

Choti and Noor turned their heads to see the oncoming chamchas. They were the same men who had held Anarkali down so Raja could shoot her. Choti's heart beat against her ribs, Raja would not be far behind.

Noor stood up and said, "Reporter Rekha, I can take Choti to my ashram. No one will think she's there, and I doubt these thugs would think to enter a place filled with grieving, white-clad widows. It would be very bad for their reputation if they were found harassing colorless widows. What do you think?" Noor said, quickly concealing Choti in the folds of her saree.

A POUCH OF COLOR

Rekha thought for a minute, "Yes, I think you're right. That would be the best thing, for now. Hopefully, you can keep Choti hidden enough that no one will notice and no one will find her. She needs to be completely invisible," Rekha said, causing Choti to bite her lip. "After the storm passes, we can make our next move."

Noor pointed to a very narrow alley full of people. Choti and Rekha quickly followed her through the twisting color-filled alleys toward her ashram. Noor chose a particularly complicated route determined to throw the policemen off their track.

Noor stopped briefly at the ashram gate. "Rekha, this is a widow's ashram," Noor said. "No family or friends of any kind are allowed in. That is a terrible sin. It will get me in a lot of trouble if I'm caught. *Par Bhagwan ki kripa hai toh*—But god willing, I will be able to sneak Choti in."

Rekha nodded, touched Choti's forehead as a blessing, and left the two of them in front of the ashram.

"Wait here, Choti, just pretend you are like any of the other kids playing in the street," Noor said, pushing at the gate. "I have to make sure no one is around to see us. When everyone is deep in prayer in the courtyard during the prayer session, I will sneak you in."

Play like any other child? Choti didn't really know how to play, for as long as she could remember, she had always worked to stay alive.

Choti walked a few meters away from the gate and came across a group of children about her age who were laughing and shrieking and already spraying colored water and spewing colored powder all over one another, making a rainbow of a mess all over their faces and bodies. But Choti didn't want to or really know how to join in the children's joyous, unabashed, Holi play (they would have probably chased her off or beat her if she tried to). Her real intention was to steal a plastic pouch of their lovely colored powder. And when the children were too busy smearing each other with color to notice, that's exactly what she did, darting in and out in her truest Varanasi tamashaist-beggar form, to retrieve a small packet of Maharani pink gulal, without drawing so much as a blink from the other children, who obviously had become colorblind.

Now Choti had her powder—Noor's powder. She tucked it inside the pocket of the flowered frock Noor had sewn for her and returned to the ashram, where she saw Noor, after she had done her tulsi watering and circumambulation, waving at her from a balcony.

Noor mutely traced a path in the air to inform Choti about the route she should take. Choti slipped in as directed through the still open gate, crept across the edge of the courtyard, circled back around the courtyard, and found herself gingerly scaling the steps that led to Noor's tiny shared accommodation. Her time on the tight-rope had really paid off. No one noticed Choti infiltrate the sanctity of Noor's ashram.

Choti's eyes, which for most of her young life had mostly seen the tops of expectant bobbing heads and the insides of flimsy and ephemeral cardboard boxes, now took in the interior of Noor's room, which seemed to Choti like the most worn-out room in the most worn-out building in the world—windowless, gloomy, and damp, with paint peeling off the cracked and dilapidated walls, whose only decorations were pictures of gods from age-old calendars.

If Anarkali, rest in peace, had imbued Choti with anything, it was a sense of humor almost impervious to any circumstances. She slipped her feet out of the slippers of fading blue—that had now become a muted gray—and politely left them outside her widow friend's door.

Noor appeared silently from her room and said in a hushed whisper: "Girl, use your head, bring your slippers inside! No one can know you are here."

Choti did as Noor instructed and immediately retrieved her slippers and brought them into the tiny, spartan room. Noor took the slippers and slid them under her sleeping mat, then quietly closed the door.

"Noor, a promise is a promise, even in the worse circumstances," Choti said, reaching into her frock's pocket.

"Huh?" Noor said, barely paying attention as she nervously inspected the room for even the smallest possible clues of her new guest's presence.

Choti pulled out the pouch of pink powder and put it in her palm.

Noor gasped in disbelief.

"Your favorite color," Choti said, beaming.

Noor accepted the pack from Choti and tossed it onto Asha's bed. "It's best not to discuss that just yet," Noor said, and cleared her throat. "Choti, child, please, no games for now, just stay as quiet as possible, try not to even move around. Any creak in the floor can set the other widows off to gossip and spy. Especially my roommate, Asha."

Choti lowered her voice and tiptoed closer to Noor.

"You have a roommate?" Choti asked.

Noor placed her finger to her lips. "Shhh. Relax. I will get you some rice." Noor made sure to wrap her Tagore book in plastic before taking it with her to the kitchen. Choti watched from the window as Noor quietly stepped out and going behind the mango tree, hid her book in a hole in the wall.

A few moments later, Noor quietly slipped back into her room with a bowl of rice for Choti—and suddenly realized how shocking it would be to everyone if they knew that she had dared sneak in a child from the streets, whom she had randomly met at the ghats one day. Now this same girl was sitting on her own sleeping mat in the petal-covered frock she had taken the time and risk to stitch for her. Noor breathed in deeply, trying to calm herself as she fought back tears and tried to find the right words for it all.

"Ahhhh, my Buntter Ply," was all Noor could muster under the quiet pressure of the room

Choti had to swallow her giggles whole. "Buntter Ply," Choti said, mimicking Noor, and they both laughed under their breath, bent over and holding their stomachs, which themselves suddenly seemed to flutter.

Noor sat beside her secret new guest on her meager bedding and began to finger-feed Choti some rice, bite-by-bite, as if she was her own daughter, the daughter she never had. As she swallowed each mouthful of bland rice, Choti's body was suffused with warmth, and her cheeks grew flushed. It was the first time she felt like she belonged somewhere and to someone, that she was loved and cared for by someone. For those few moments, Choti felt absolute peace, as her stomach purred through the butterflies for more rice.

"When I grow up and start to fly, I promise I will take care of you," Choti said, between bites and swallows. "Even if that means never getting married and taking a job I hate, it will always be you and me flying together, Ma."

Noor began to weep silently. She held Choti in her arms and hugged her close. "Everyone wishes to die in Varanasi to escape from the cycles of birth and rebirth. But I don't want Moksha, Choti, I don't want Moksha. I want another chance at life. We will both leave Varanasi tonight. I have never ever been on the other side of the Ganga…"

"I know, we can go to Tagore's home," Choti said excitedly.

"No, I'll take you to Kolkata to my hometown and send you to school," Noor said her face shining.

Choti set her bowl of rice aside and hugged Noor back and said, "Can I call you Ma then?"

Noor's roommate Asha had been watching both of them the whole time. She had watched their arrival at the gate, she had watched the stranger conferring with them and then leaving abruptly, she had watched Choti run off to "play" with the children, she had watched Noor wave her directions from the balcony.

And what did Asha do after so much watching but immediately call the police to make a report, as she had overheard on the streets that they were searching for Choti over the murder of Anarkali.

In no time at all Choti and Noor heard the clamor of footsteps and resonating voices rushing up the ashram stairs.

"Choti, listen to me, crawl in as deep under Asha's bed as you can and make yourself as quiet and small as possible. Hurry!" Noor rushed around the room, trying to hide the Holi powder and any other trace of Choti's presence.

But it was too late. The door whipped open and there stood, fuming in a collective glare, Asha surrounded by Raja's chamchas. Asha barged into the room, not even bothering to take her shoes off as she trod all over Noor's sleeping mat, and pierced every corner of the room with her eyes, which had become sharp as razors.

"Noor, how many times have I warned you to stay out of trouble? And now you have brought all this trouble back to the ashram," Asha intoned.

"Asha, I thought you were my friend. Has the world changed, or have we changed?" Noor said. "How could you do this to me?"

"Noor, you've becoming a sinner," Asha said, showing no mercy. "That's how I could."

Noor stood frozen in place, saying nothing, like a sad, humiliated child, accepting her punishment, with no defense but a puzzled frown. It was a wonder all the blood from her heart didn't burst out and spill onto the white surface of her saree.

"You are a sinner," Asha said. "You are against the Gods, you are against religion, you are against society. You are against everything!"

A POUCH OF COLOR

The police goons trickled in on either side of Asha, rubbing their knuckles, adjusting their belts, smoothing their mustaches, readying for violence.

Noor took a breath and found the strength to speak. "Saving a life is not against any form of religion I know of."

One of Choti's feet poked out from under Asha's bed, and the bulging eye of the ugliest, dourest-faced chamcha saw it. Chaos ensued as the chamcha reached down and caught Choti's foot like it was the tail of a Ganga fish being pulled from a net. "I knew it," Asha said, smirking. "You've stained the ashram with another sinner, and under my own bed, Noor! The gods will never forgive you."

The chamcha showed no mercy in pulling Choti first by the legs and then more violently by grabbing her by her hair. Choti kicked and threw her fists, even spat in the chamcha's face. "You smelly little fish!" said the chamcha.

"Leave me alone. I didn't see anything. Noor, help me, Noor!" begged Choti.

Noor deployed every limb of her withered body against the goons. Hitting them with her weak fists and finally throwing herself at their feet. "She's just a child, leave her alone! She's not a danger to anybody! Don't fear her, fear the Gods!" Noor shouted until she was hoarse.

All the ashram's widows collected in the courtyard, gathering like a white fog, sweeping closer to the veranda to witness the tamasha and hearken to Noor's screams— "Leave her alone! Let her go! She is sick and in danger, the girl will die if I don't take care of her!"

The chamchas beat Noor back and pushed her back into her room, where another oily haired, paan chewing chamcha lingered. He stepped onto the veranda, next to where Asha had rushed to position herself. "The girl is finished," the chamcha said, drawing his finger across his throat and whistling. "She shouldn't have raised her voice against the Lead Inspector. She did, and now the girl is as good as dead."

As soon as the police had left with their child captive, Asha leaned over the veranda to spread word of Noor's sins.

"I've personally witnessed this widow's excesses with my own eyes. She has no shame! I've seen her drinking sugared chai," Asha said.

The other women in the ashram began taunting Noor:

"If you are so keen to have a daughter, then get married and produce one of your own…"

"We renounced all our earthly ties and came here to spend our time in prayer and worship, and this loose woman is having a roaring time…"

"The slut! She's at death's door but still wants a good time…"

Asha reached over and yanked up Noor's saree to expose her foot. "And look at this! She dares even to put nail polish on her toes to seduce the new husband obsessing her mind! She's destroyed the sanctity of this ashram for widows by treating it like an ashram for married couples."

"It's a sin, it's a sin," the widows began to whisper in chorus, reacting to each other's growing shock.

"And this young new 'bride' even plans to play Holi with that young girl she regards as her own flesh and blood daughter," Asha continued, displaying the pouch of bright

A POUCH OF COLOR

pink pigment she had found under her bed. All the widows present shut their eyes to avoid their own sin of looking at color.

Noor made a grab for the pouch—the proof of her sinful desire, and also her love for Choti, the closest thing to a daughter she'd ever had.

All the women gathered in the veranda closed in further and began to harangue Noor. Noor was cornered, pushed to the end of the terrace: "Shame, shame, shame," they repeated until Noor was forced to cover her ears. She looked through the widows' crowding presence and saw Choti being dragged out of the ashram's front entrance.

Noor screamed, "Choti, my darling child, fight them, try to run and never look back, you are big, one day you will fly above them all!"

At this point Asha lunged at Noor to intimidate her, and Noor took a couple of hasty steps back. She missed her footing and fell off the ledge of the first-floor veranda, hitting her head hard on the courtyard tiles.

It took that kind of violent action to convince the widows, including Asha, to finally cease their aggression.

Blood flowed from her head like a vermilion river, but Noor never got to see its brilliant hue. Would the other widows dare ever recall its color after it flowed past the tulsi plant Noor had nurtured every day with Ganga water?

Noor died while still clutching a pouch of sinful, vivid pink, a pouch of color she never had the chance to open.

Why do I threaten you?
You have a million weapons, I only have truth

Why are you cremating me?
You have the entire Sun, I only have the light of hope
Why are you burying me?
You have the entire Earth, I only have a puff of dust
Why are you drowning me?
You have an entire River, I barely exist in a drop of water

The beasts in police garb dragged Choti by her hair out of the ashram to Ganga herself. Then they blindfolded her and dumped her in a police patrol motorboat. She heard the engine start, and go faster and faster, racing along the ghats, steering away towards sinister darker waters. She felt a warm breeze on her face. *But she wasn't on her tightrope. Where was the safe and clear height of her air? And where was Noor?*

Choti had never learned how to swim. Why? Because she had always been an aerial creature, walking the tightrope high in the sky, or in a tree concealed in her sky-nest.

She wanted to fly, but she had to drown to meet Anarkali again.

Choti heard one of the officer's say, "Drown her in the river, this stupid girl is creating too much trouble. It will be a clean end of the Anarkali case if we just push her in."

Her hands were bound with rope and then suddenly one of the men grabbed her with his rough dirty hands and cast her over the side of the speeding boat into Ganga's fast waters.

But did they release her? No, they did not. They held onto her by her hair. She sank into the filthy water and splashed her arms around trying to stay above the surface to catch her breath, but all she felt was more pressure on her hair. It hurt so much, she wished her scalp would just tear off and they would just let her drown. To sink to the bottom of the river with the big fish and dead bodies that choked it.

Choti stopped fighting and closed her eyes, and then her frail limp child's body began to float, lapped by the dark of Ganga's waters.

The boat stopped and abruptly Choti was pulled back in. Raja's henchmen carried her wrapped in a thin blanket back into Nagar Nigam Station, where her whole ordeal had first begun.

Was Choti dead?

No, the wretched child clung as stubbornly to life as she had as a newborn. Ten years ago, abandoned in a garbage tip, with no air in her lungs, the infant Choti had been rescued by the Woman in a Yellow Saree, and survived. This time too, though her lungs were full of water, Choti spluttered, and her frail body shook and shivered and slowly wakened to life.

"Don't put her back in," one of the men implored. "We've been dunking the kid in water for half an hour. Obviously, Ganga Ma doesn't want her dead and if we mess with this child, the Goddess will take us to task…"

The police station was unusually busy, full of petty criminals, aggrieved people trying to lodge their complaints, and cops going about their business. Chintu sat in a far corner with handcuffs on his hands. The already skinny child had lost more weight. The smile had gone from his face. His eyes were dull and glazed. He had just spent almost a year in jail for some petty crime and was being released that day. He had been sentenced without trial. A young child thrown into the dungeons with hardened criminals just because he had shouted at one of the men he was gambling with, and had lost his money to, turned out to be a friend of Raja's.

Suddenly there was a commotion in the hall as a couple of policemen burst in carrying a small girl wrapped in a blanket.

Filthy water dripped all over the desk and floor of the holding room.

Chintu stared in shock as he caught a glimpse of the girl's face!

Just then Raja rushed in, beaming with excitement. "Excellent. I see you've given this little guttersnipe a fine lesson in police procedure and how to become a more responsible citizen of Varanasi," he said. "Take her downstairs immediately and finish the job. That's an order!"

Then the officer who had stopped her drowning before, one of Raja's subordinates called Veer, who was fresh, younger, brighter-eyed than the rest, dared approach to offer his opinion.

"Please sir, you can't torture this child anymore, she's had enough! We did everything we could to finish her off; we keel-hauled her in the Ganga, I was there and it was terrible. The men did their best, but she survived."

Raja's eyes appeared to sear the fresh-faced officer alive but he insisted on finishing what he had to say:

"Sir, I promise you, I saw it with my own eyes, I saw Ganga Ma give the girl her breath back. It was a miracle," the young officer insisted. "She's Ganga's own daughter. The right thing to do is release her, otherwise it will prove certain bad luck for all of us."

"Shut up! This is my station and what I say, goes, understood?" Raja said imperiously. "Ganga's own daughter, eh?" he stroked his chin. He was worried that Choti and the reporter woman could get him into serious trouble and wanted them out of the scene permanently. "We'll see about that."

Veer tried to reason with his superior once more: "Sir, please sir, she's just a child."

Raja grabbed him by the collar and shoved him hard against the wall. "I suggest you worry about your own children! If you don't follow my orders you might be the one who ends up at the bottom of the Ganga."

Chintu watched in horror as Choti was taken downstairs.

The Flower of Faded Orange

A heritage of a book and a paper flower

Rekha had been haunting the colorful streets of Varanasi, drinking chai, pacing, brooding, biding her time. Finally, nerve-racking anxiety had driven her back to the ashram to do a little spying. Immediately she knew something was amiss. She saw that a small group of local women of all ages, old and wrinkled, young and still smooth-faced, decked-out in rich Varanasi textiles with their heads covered, had gathered at the gate, their attention riveted across it.

Though she badly wanted to, Rekha could not barge into the courtyard like the intrepid journalist she was, because only widowed women were allowed to enter—and she wasn't even married yet. The local women kept up a constant murmur of whispered curiosity as they stared across the gate at the ashram. She moved closer to them to hear what they were saying.

"Can you believe it, now these widows are adopting children?" one of the women said.

"Shame! Soon these inauspicious crones, whose dark shadow caused the death of their husbands, will invade our whole society," said another.

"Thank God the police took action and arrested that little thief of a street girl," a third woman said.

Rekha's face turned pale with horror. "Did you see what happened?" she asked them.

The women all nodded. "*Everyone* saw it. Such audacity! Shame on them, shame."

"What did everyone see?" Rekha persisted.

"They dragged that dirty little thief girl out of the ashram by her hair!"

Rekha's heart sank. The worst that she had feared had happened. She placed her hand on her chest to calm her loudly beating heart. "And? What else did you see?"

"Then an old widow fell off the veranda, hit her head, and died on the spot. She must have been the guilty one who let the streetchild in."

All the life seemed to be knocked out of Rekha's body. She clutched weakly at the wall behind her as a wave of nausea convulsed her body.

"The worst part of it all…"

"Yes, yes, what was it?" another woman in the crowd asked eagerly, taking great pleasure in the tragedy that had just occurred.

"…was that the old widow clutched a packet of pink gulal in her hands."

The crowd gasped in collective disapproval of such blatantly blasphemous behavior.

THE FLOWER OF FADED ORANGE

Rekha raced back to Nagar Nigam, arriving at the police station's front desk, in a completely hysterical state. Seeing her, the cops hanging about swiftly retreated behind their desks. One of them stood smoking and staring—*here was the reporter lady from Delhi again, come to stir up more trouble,* he was thinking, no doubt.

"Where's the inspector on duty?" Rekha demanded to know. "I want to speak to him immediately!"

The inspector on duty stepped to the desk, but Rekha didn't recognize him, and he just ignored her and pretended to study some case files on the desk, while keeping his eyes on a phone he pretended to expect to ring any second with some urgent call that would surely demand his serious attention.

"Inspector! Listen to me. Did your officers bring a young girl in today?" Rekha said. "I've been looking for her. If she's here you could be in serious trouble."

The inspector didn't even look up from his files.

Rekha raised her voice loud enough so that even the cops in the back offices and cells must have heard it. "Answer me! Did anyone bring Choti in? I demand to know. Let me tell you all, there will be serious ramifications, if even an inch on her body is hurt."

At the far end of the desk, Rekha spied a scrap of faded orange, now with flecks of deep red criss-crossing it, and it seemed like it had become damp and had then been dried out. It was the flower from Choti's hair. Her eyes widened and she threw up her arms, as she raced to the end of the desk in a rage, and snatched up the flower. Brandishing it at all of them she said, "I know she's here. I'm not going away until I get justice. I'm going to call the Delhi Police Department and the Security Ministry and report to all the ministers that the UP police have abducted a juvenile witness to a cover up a murder committed by its very own officers."

The inspector at the desk laughed in her face. "So, now a journalist thinks she can determine the fate of a police officer," he said, his gaze resting lecherously on her chest. "Madamji, I'm sure you realize that hundreds of people are openly cremated here on the ghat, every single day. Get your nose out of official police business and buy a bus ticket back to Delhi before you become an earthenware pot yourself."

The other cops laughed with him in open mockery.

Rekha banged the desk again. "Sir, I've made it my duty to bring the world's attention to the crimes your corrupt force has committed. And there are many. Where is Inspector Raja?"

Raja suddenly strode through the entrance and stood behind Rekha, exhaling his foul breath. "I'm right here," he said, targeting his harsh whisper into Rekha's ear.

Rekha turned to face him.

"Journalist lady from Delhi, I could kill you and bury you in the station's backyard and no one would even know about it. Do yourself a favor, either forget about this and go enjoy Holi like everyone else, or go back to Delhi and save your life. The pyres of Manikarnika burn all evidence of life away. Even your ashes mingle with those of a thousand others. No one will ever be able to trace what happened to you."

"But you murdered Anarkali in cold blood! How can you stand there like nothing happened?" Rekha said.

"Keep your voice low," Raja rasped.

"I will do quite the opposite, I know people in the ministry and the media. They all know where I am, and what I'm investigating. Don't you dare threaten me! Now that I know you've abducted Choti as well."

Raja dropped his lids across his cold, dead eyes. Rekha stared the inspector down.

"I promise you, the world will hear of this, Raja," said Rekha.

Raja grabbed hold of Rekha's wrist like he was cuffing it. "You have no proof of any of this. I own these streets of Varanasi," he said. Raja yanked Rekha to the door and shoved her out. "Stop sticking your nose in official police business and allow us to continue doing our best work for the people of Varanasi," Raja said, continuing to bully Rekha down the street, as tears of rage streamed down her cheeks at the sheer malice in his voice.

Raja waited for Rekha to leave and then instructed his men, "Take the little guttersnipe to the men's jail near the police gym; that reporter bitch should not know where she is."

Chintu, who had been listening all along, cowering in a corner, knew what the first thing was he had to do when he was released.

Raja strode into the police chambers near the akhara, the wrestlers' pit, and looked into one cell in particular. Seated among a few drugged-out men, was a wan and shivering, broken-bodied young girl in a torn and dirty flowered dress, who lay crumpled in the corner like an old rag. The bright petals that had once adorned the dress had long since wilted.

Raja banged his stick on the cell's encrusted bars. "Eh you! Street-rat, widow-thief, so who was it who killed Anarkali again?"

Choti was too weak to answer.

Raja took out his keys and opened the overcrowded cell. He kicked and waved his stick through the other prisoners towards Choti. All of them moved to the corners of the cell.

Choti, experiencing for the first time the real terror of a child, was energized by pure fear to jump up and then cower against the cell's furthest wall, like a chicken, ready to be slaughtered.

"I don't know anything, Babuji," she whispered. "I'm sorry, I won't say anything. I promise. Anarkali? Who is this Anarkali you keep talking about? Please, Babuji let me go to my old mother, Noor. Please have mercy. Please just take me to Noor."

Raja shoved his stick into Choti's ribs, and she screamed and fluttered her arms in panic. "If you don't know anything, then why are you so scared?" Raja said.

The other prisoners stirred in their dark corners, and Raja threw all of them a threatening look. "Shut up! Or you're all next!" Raja said, and they immediately grew still again.

Raja called out to Veer. "You, keep an eye on this gutter rat!" Raja said.

Choti's eyes glazed over, as if they no longer connected the outside world to her inner person; as if she had already left her corporeal self. Raja flicked Choti's damp, blood-crusted head. "But first shave off her hair," the king of Varanasi said, and grinned.

In the evening, Rekha sat on the same bench near Tulsi Ghat where she had first found Choti, frantically scrawling in her notebook, and, as much as her concern would allow her to, occasionally looking up to observe what seemed like all of Varanasi's population lighting and holding aloft their trays of golden lit candles, and heading for Ganga's shore in celebration of aarti in all its flickering, flaming, reverent and quiet glory.

Rekha knew Choti was being detained in Raja's police custody without legitimacy or documentation, but after Raja threw her into the street, and she tried to return (she couldn't help herself) to Nagar Nigam to get more information about Choti's whereabouts, she was repeatedly scuttled away under threat of her life.

Now she was making calls to everyone she knew; she had got one of the reporters in her office to talk to a local woman's organization, she had phoned the MLA of Varanasi district and threatened to put the story in the papers. She was doing everything she could but she could do nothing if they hurt Choti.

If Choti was dead, what would she do?

Suddenly a small boy wearing a cap with a check-mark on it walked over and disturbed Rekha's frantic note-taking. "Are you from Delhi for Anarkali's case?" the boy said.

"Yes, I am, but who wants to know?" Rekha said, a little on edge.

"I know where they have taken her, and we need to help her. Please come with me, we have to go there now, it's urgent…"

Rekha looked at the boy. "Who are you?" she said.

The boy's eyes moistened, though his upturned chin still indicated his street-hardened pride. "My name is Chintu. I am Choti's friend and partner."

Choti woke up in a strange cell, barely conscious and still bleeding, with water dripping down her face. Her memory of things was fuzzy. Blood had dried across the smeared petals of her frock, tears she didn't remember crying had crusted around her eyes, bruises and welts stiffened her limbs, she was damp and her hair was gone, cut short as a boy's, like bloody Chintu's, just another sign of the spirit they had dragged out of her.

She stared at the leaking ceiling, inhaled the foul odor, and heard the voices of talking women. Was she still at the ashram? *Noor? Ma, are you still here?* she thought, and nearly asked aloud.

Then she remembered a man beating the soles of her ankles with his stick, as he yelled, "You used to walk a tight-rope, now you won't even be able to walk on the ground. And by the way that sinful old woman Noor is dead, I thought I should let you know…"

Choti recalled what the man had told her and broke down. It was the news of Noor's death that had made her lose consciousness, not the beatings. Her heart cried out for Noor, for Anarkali, for Chintu… *where are all my friends, somebody help me, please, I'm so tired, I miss you, I need you, please Ganga Ma I don't want to die…*

Choti was overcome by all the memories and collapsed in a huddle on the floor.

The day of Holi arrived. Mists of pigment flung into the air by boisterous Holi players blocked out even the acrid smoke of Manikarnika. Cremations in Varanasi would be a different kind of cremation that day, not just of bodies into ash or bodies into water, but of burning emotion and playful forgiveness exploding into a full spectrum of a joyous frenzy of color. *Holi Hai! Holi Hai!* many in Varanasi wanted to say, and most of them would, as they attacked one another with pigments and gulal of every color and hue, leaving behind trails of laughter and happiness.

All would be forgiven, except the few, the wretched and the damned of Varanasi.

That Holi morning, the Varanasi sun remained stubbornly at Ganga's horizon, which appeared gray and somehow drained of its fire, before finally making its proud, bright ascent, and everyone became festive again. Holi had arrived.

At the ashram, the widows prepared for Noor's funeral. They had already dressed her in a saree of pure white, covered her face and head with it, and were now placing her body on a funeral bier. Usually when one widow died, the other widows would chant praises for the Lord's protection and passage, but for Noor there was only silence.

Asha found the need to run from widow to widow proclaiming: "I'm glad Noor died alone. It was for the best. Imagine if we had allowed her to keep this 'daughter' or her shameful pink toes, how many sins she would have stained our holy tradition and community with."

Having caused the accident that led to her death she now wanted everyone to believe that Noor was truly, absolutely evil and deserved to die.

"Asha's right. Shame, shame!" the widows chanted, until one of them raised her arms, closed her eyes, and looked at the lightening sky to scream out, "Devi Ma, forgive her, she faced her life on this earth with great penance and fortitude. Ma Ganga, grant her Moksha."

"She won't be. That I know. Shame, shame!" Asha retorted.

"Shame, Shame!" the other widows chanted as they went back to preparing Noor for her final journey.

The Bird Flies

Broken wings, buried seeds,
eclipsed sun

When Choti fainted in Raja's jail cell, the men there started shrieking because they thought she was dead. Upon hearing the shrieks, Veer entered the cell and saw Choti lying on the floor, barely conscious. Not knowing what else to do he picked her up off the ground, and sprinkled some water on her face.

She looked up at him weakly.

"Can you stand?" Veer asked in a kind voice.

With great difficulty, the broken-bodied Choti stood up.

Veer steadied her by gripping her elbow. "You need to go to the bathroom and wash up; you'll feel better that way."

Choti became slowly aware of a hazy distant hum of voices—people wishing one other Holi.

As they walked down the long corridor Veer told Choti in a hushed whisper, "Look, I'm sorry about how you've been treated. Your friend Chintu got in touch with me and told me to give you this." He handed her a thin length of rope, as fragile as a washing line, but it was her only hope. "Chintu and that journalist lady are waiting for you. The bathroom has a skylight. Best of luck and now go…this is your only chance…I can't help you again…"

"Chintu?" Choti barely understood what was happening, but she went into the bathroom and locked the door from inside. She looked at herself in the stained mirror. Her reflection told her what she already knew, that she was in bad shape but at least she was still alive. That fact alone gave her renewed energy; as did the words that Noor had always said to her; that one day she would "fly."

Choti looked up and saw a small high—cracked-open—window up near the bathroom's ceiling.

Choti considered the floor, the ceiling, and the open window, and had no option but to make a silent prayer and start her climb, a climb she hoped would lead her first to Noor and then to freedom. A new determination burned through her. She held the rope Chintu had sent for her and shimmied up an iron sewage pipe (it reminded her of her tight-rope stick) jutting through the bathroom floor and reaching up to and out of the window.

Choti gripped the pipe with her hands and feet and began to climb, slowly but steadily until her face glowed with a small square of the afternoon sun's warming light. And before she had the chance to feel any pain from her injured feet or Ganga-tortured body, she gingerly appeared, light as a bird flying from its cage, on the terrace above the station overlooking the wrestling pit where she had first seen Anarkali being murdered.

She looked across her black and white city of death, suddenly reincarnating in full color, with all of Varanasi now being painted in the many colors of Holi. Choti took a deep breath, almost trying to breathe-in and fill herself with the glorious hues of every color she saw, then began to climb from terrace to terrace, until she felt far enough away from Nagar Nigam and Raja and his potbellied chamchas, to feel, at least momentarily, "safe," if safety was even possible in Varanasi. Then she tied the rope to the side of a pipe and gently let herself down.

When Raja's on-duty police discovered that Choti had escaped, they fanned out on foot and motorcycle in all different directions looking for her. Word of Choti's fortunate escape soon spread to Rekha and Chintu's ears—the two had been keeping up a dedicated vigil near the police station as they considered what to do next. They too fanned out to cover the area, looking for Choti.

Two of Raja's goons ran to Raja's home to inform him about Choti's escape. They arrive in the midst of Raja's family performing a Holi puja. Upon the interruption, Raja lost his temper and began yelling at the top of his voice, "You good for nothing people! You lazy bastards! You call yourself police? You can't even control a little girl. How could she escape? Were you sleeping with your faces in the dregs of your tea? I am going to fire the whole department."

"A little girl? Why is the entire police force trying to capture and kill a little girl?" Rani asked.

"Shut up and mind your own business, or your little girls will suffer the same fate!"

Raja's bulging eyes and livid screaming sent his daughters back into their room, and their father continued to yell as he left the puja, and ran to his room to change into his uniform. His wife Rani followed her furious husband into their bedroom to help him dress.

As Raja fought with the buttons on his shirt, Rani, having spied Raja's gun holster on the bed, silently reached over to remove Raja's gun and empty the bullets, before putting it back.

When Raja's men came to pick him up, Rani spoke out for the first time, knowing that they too would hear what she had to say: "Say, Raja, do you know why I never touched the waters at Lolark Kund? Do you know why I never prayed for a son?"

Raja tried to ease the situation by sheepishly glancing around at his boys, then fell into a shocked, staring silence, his eyes becoming like black darts into his wife's soul, as she shrieked, "I never wanted to give birth to a Ravana like your mother did!"

Raja seized his wife's flailing arms, but she continued: "Raja, one day a daughter will rise to crush you and everything you stand for. Before then, I curse you. I curse you."

Held aloft by the hands of the other widows, Noor's body departed through the ashram's gate on a funeral bier and was carried through the narrow streets toward Manikarnika Ghat. Raja's police, expecting Choti would appear, had filled in any gaps between the widow's death parade and the intricate networks of streets on either side, front and behind. If she appeared, she would be theirs.

THE BIRD FLIES

Choti zigzagged the streets as she sought to evade capture, catching glimpses from around corners and rooftops and stairways of her and Noor's favorite spots, especially their bench on the hidden terrace. As she snuck from place to place, still not quite sure where she was going, she saw the children from the Nameless House with Pink Walls, who had again dressed up as the Hindu pantheon of gods and goddesses for Holi, being interrogated by a handful of Raja's potbellies, under threat of having their masks ripped from their faces.

Then Choti saw a procession. Noor's body, wrapped in a white saree, floated and teetered and moved atop a flow of hands toward Manikarnika. Around the procession, walked or stood groups of police. Obviously, they were not interested in an old dead widow.

Choti had come around the sharp corner of an alley when she saw an irresistible eyeful, a huge pile of pink gulal pigment. She feigned to speed past the Holi stand, but as she did, and before anyone noticed, she swooped her hand in to swipe a large handful of the glowing pigment into the pocket of her frock.

Right near the last turn before Manikarnika, Choti stopped to drink water from a sprung pipe. When she cupped her hands, the pooled water reflected back a disc that looked like the moon. Perhaps the moon had been hiding in her hands the whole time, ready to eclipse that which sought to burn her. Over the small reflected moon, Choti closed her eyes and made a small, vague prayer for Noor, asking that she would not suffer and would have safe passage to somewhere, a somewhere that would last forever.

Choti threw the moon from her hands, and ran up the rickety exposed staircase of an abandoned house into a door. She locked the door behind her, and ran up another set of stairs to the building's collapsing terrace—and who did she see appear out of nowhere in the dimness across the way on the opposite terrace but a miracle of the gods themselves, her glorious bloody thief of a partner, Chintu and the journalist auntie!

Choti had no time to consider whether it was really Chintu or just some hopeful phantasm desperately risen from her desperate imagination, but then Chintu was throwing a tight-rope across the sky for her to catch. The journalist auntie was praying hard, her hands folded, her eyes shut, so worried that Choti might hurt herself.

On the second try, Choti caught the rope and then Chintu pointed his fingers in his usual V-shape, first at his eyes, then at Choti's, then back to his again, and they both smiled.

This was no time for Choti to grudge Chintu a couple of stolen bucks.

Choti tied her end of the rope firmly to a pole, then tested its tautness with her feet to ensure it could hold her weight. On the opposite terrace, Chintu was having no such luck. He could find no pole to tie his end of the rope to. He flashed his V-sign again at Choti, who flashed her own V-sign back, as Chintu sat firmly on the ground after wrapping the rope around his body and arms like a giant constricting snake, and dropping all his weight to earth, braced his feet on the roughened edge of the terrace,

THE BIRD FLIES

then reared as mightily as a boy his size could. The rope seemed to hold fast, bouncing up with surprising tautness, but it was surely a blessing and a good thing Choti was so feather-light and small, with hollow bones like a bird.

Noor's procession rounded the corner of Chintu and Choti's newly rope-spanned alley, as Choti began her slow walk, gaining her old balance and momentum as she always did, ignoring the blood oozing from her injured feet.

Then she felt it. She was the moon, the small thing, eclipsing the spring sun. Choti's shadow cast across the procession of widows below and everyone looked up in stunned astonishment, just like Noor had said they would one day. Then she saw Noor directly below, peacefully arranged on her funeral bier, ready to be fed to the flames of Manikarnika Ghat. Perhaps it was Choti's wishful imagination but she swore she could see her old widow friend Noor smile.

Balancing above all the heads, not caring if she lived or died, she reached into her frock's pocket, grabbed a fistful of pink and threw it straight onto Noor! The magical forgiving powder saturated Noor with her favorite color, a color the widow, for almost her entire life could never admit, and the same color Choti imagined Rajasthani queens danced and twirled in.

Some who witnessed all the color suddenly splashed onto Noor's saree, which also drew attention to Noor's still pink-painted toes, might have seen the spectacle as an example of the lowest, vilest sin (would they have preferred blood or the dirty ashes of burned bones?) but to Choti it was the purest heaven on earth, a heaven as splendid as the sun rising over the Ganga.

It was the seeking of that lasting and heavenly image that drove Choti's legs, injured and tired as they were, deftly across the edge of the rope.

The burst of sudden pink, which had arrived like a bomb of color dropped from above, caught the attention of Raja, who had just made his way through the throng of chamchas and widows, already gripping his holster at the scene. When Raja reached for his gun and aimed it at the little child the whole crowd saw him in his true colors. Surely her sin was not *that* big, they thought.

He pulled the trigger of the unloaded gun again and again, screaming in frustration as the little urchin evaded him, cheating death once more, because with her was the protection of Ganga Ma and the guiding spirits of Noor and Anarkali.

As she finished her tight-rope act in a blaze of color, Chintu and Rekha pulled her to safety. Rekha gathered her in her arms and hugged her tight and said, "Hurry child, I have a car waiting. My colleagues are waiting in a back alley. Chintu knows the way."

They ran all the way down to an Ambassador car waiting for them further up. Choti and Rekha climbed in and before she could say anything, Chintu gave her a hug.

"Aren't you coming with me?" Choti asked.

"My world is here, Choti, this is the only one I know," Chintu grinned, and rushed into the swell of people all around, instantly vanishing in the burst of crowds and color and the happy hopeful shouts of *"Holi Hai!"*

Epilogue

Varanasi, Holi Day, March 2012

From bright colors to the last color of ash

She had gathered all the widows in the dilapidated sun-bleached, time-worn ashram to prepare to celebrate Holi. But, when they had all been coaxed out of their cells—a task in itself—her colleagues, Alka and Geeta, informed her that a swelling horde of locals, security officers and police had barged in through the ashram's gate and had seized the courtyard to try to keep the widows from enjoying their first-ever Holi celebration.

"You've come all the way from Delhi for this, Noor Saxena. What is our next step going to be?" Alka asked her pointedly.

Noor, aka Choti, touched the jute shoulder bag on her arm. In it, next to the Supreme Court Order, lay that most precious thing: the book of Tagore, that Noor's grandfather had given her, and which she had, with her infinite spirit presence, found a way to guide her toward; helping her instinctively locate the magical pink book in a secret cubbyhole in the brick wall.

She looked Alka in the eye and replied: "I am going to ensure these women get their Supreme Court-ordered freedom to further 'sin' and 'destroy' their culture with their own hands: I will help them grab fistfuls of gulal, of rose-pink and earth-red, and throw the color into the sky, I'll help them play Holi in joyful abandon with their friends... as I had promised twenty years ago."

Alka grabbed her elbow. "Noor, the crowd outside is saying that if the widows even *begin* to play Holi, it will destroy everyone's values and culture, not to mention condemning them all to hell," she said.

Filled with a confidence that could only have been derived from her having transcended her own namelessness, powerlessness, and inferiority—the same transcendence she so desperately wanted every widow in India to experience—she strode with bold steps toward the ashram door, with Alka and Geeta at her heels.

"Well, this time the ball is in Choti's court," she said confidently.

Noor once again stood at the same spot in the courtyard where, once, her kindest, oldest friend, with her white saree and bald head and timid manner, had risked everything—and lost her life—in order to take her in and save hers.

The same yard across which rough animal hands had subsequently dragged her by the hair and then unceremoniously, without a shred of compassion or pity, thrown her into the Ganga.

As Choti, now named Noor Saxena after the two women who had changed her life, Noor and Rekha Saxena, the

EPILOGUE

journalist who fought alongside her and finally adopted her, combated those bitter memories, a murmur rose amongst all who had gathered, *"Choti? Who is this Choti?"* they seemed to be asking.

She washed her face in the fountain on the veranda nearest the tulsi plant before going back into the ashram to face to the white-clad women, who were now fully armed with their favorite hues of gulal and Holi powder. "Come on, everyone, let's go!" she said. "Let's finally celebrate Holi, and share our joys and hopes with all of Varanasi, the entire nation, and the wider world."

Together Alka, Geeta, and she led the group of widows into the ashram's open courtyard where they were accosted by the cops and angry locals, who began to collectively admonish them:

"Look at today's world, widows will play Holi, next we will hear that they want to live a new life! We won't destroy our culture! Stop all this tamasha and get back to your ashrams."

She had known all along that the widows' Holi color revolution wouldn't come easily, but one had to start somewhere, right? Especially when facing one stubborn generation, sitting atop another, even more stubborn, even less forgiving history.

A police inspector stood outside the ashram gates with a couple of his flunkeys. The crowd thronging behind them was at least fifty people strong.

The inspector looked her up and down from top to toe, then gestured with his stick:

"*Aiy ladki*, hey girl, grab your bags and get the hell out of here…"

She looked him straight in the face and answered: "Sir, my name is Noor Saxena, I am an advocate in the High Court of Delhi. Please be civil in your speech…"

"Eh, you don't preach civility to me, get your stuff and get out; you and your kind are always looking to destroy the peace in this town…"

"We're only here to play Holi," Alka said.

The inspector looked mockingly around, "*Oh hoh!* Listen to them, so now these old widows are playing Holi? What next? Today they play Holi with colors, tomorrow they'll start wearing makeup, painting their faces with color, and soon they'll want to get married."

The inspector tried to grab her by the shoulder:

"Don't you *dare* touch me again," she pulled herself away and spat at him coldly. "Let me remind you that you are committing two crimes here. First you are violating the orders of the Honorable Supreme Court and second, according to Section 46 Class 4 Criminal Procedure Code, being a male officer you cannot touch a female…"

"Oh, *accha*, right, so now you are going to teach me the law, are you? I'll see how these old crones play Holi. If I don't grab each of them by their scrawny necks and throw them out of Varanasi I'll change my name…"

At this point, one of his junior policemen stepped forward and cautioned the inspector to hold back: "Sir, it's best for you to leave. She has orders of the Supreme Court. The national and international media are going to be here soon to cover this event."

EPILOGUE

She looked up, startled, immediately recognizing the voice with her heart. Looking into the eyes of the young policeman, she said in disbelief: "Chintu?"

Meanwhile the inspector was so baffled (did he even understand the ramifications of the day?) as to say nothing in reply, so she continued: "Perhaps, what your junior colleague is saying is too much for your brain to comprehend. Let me explain it to you once again: It will be considered a violation of the Supreme Court if anyone interrupts or interferes in this celebration."

She pulled the Supreme Court papers out of her bag and thrust them into the bewildered inspector's face.

Chintu spoke to him again, tersely this time, "Sir, let the widows celebrate. There are clear orders."

The inspector massaged his jaw and mustache for a few moments as he scanned the order.

"Sir, it's the law, sir," Chintu said again.

Finally his superior admitted defeat, folded the papers and handed them back to her and motioned to his people to leave. All the policemen left except one. He ordered the crowd to disperse. The widows were free to do as they please, and as they did, some of the onlookers—even the cop who had stayed behind—joined in the revelry...

As she watched the smiling faces of the 200-strong procession of widows, now freely walking, laughing and talking on the same streets of Varanasi she had roamed as a homeless kid, she felt like she was gazing at the most familiar face in the world, like she was gazing into a mirror.

The face looking in was Noor Saxena's, the reflection staring back was that of her ten-year-old self, Choti.

Color exploded everywhere from the dirty streets to the clear skies, across white walls and dirty walls, across the cremation ghats, and across every white saree, to forever brighten every formerly black-and-white mourning heart.

Before that day, the widows of Varanasi had never dared touched color, lest they eternally suffer in sin. Today marked an entirely new celebration, a new "legal" and "sinless" celebration that deserved to have its own name, something like Holi, but much, much more.

A festival for "the end of mourning."

Could Holi and those who celebrated it, embrace such a festival for as many generations as they had rejected it as sin? She didn't know, but for now she was tempted to believe it possible.

With everyone dancing and enjoying everything Holi had to offer, basking in its playful warfare of colors, all she wanted to do was wander off alone to the Varanasi ghats, pray, and take a dip in Ma Ganga.

Dressed in Ma's favorite Banarsi silk saree, the one reserved for special occasions, Noor Saxena strode down the steps toward Ganga Ma's shore.

With every step she descended, the name of her childhood called to her in her head. *Choti, Choti, Choti...*

Did the name represent her identity, her past or her future, she didn't know, but the name kept repeating itself, and in a voice that wasn't her own. Was it Noor calling to her through everyone's joined voices? She didn't know.

EPILOGUE

But then, as the knelt by the Ganga, the setting sun burnishing the gold border of her saree, she felt touched by a special light. Basking in this, she felt the warmest presence she had ever experienced. Warmer, softer, sweeter than the gentle winter rays of that same sun, which, once a long time ago, as Noor had predicted, she would eclipse.

She turned toward the presence and thought she saw a flashing image of her old friend. First, she saw a vision of her alone on their terrace bench waving to her, and then suddenly her friend Noor was dancing in the midst of a colored cloud of her favorite pink hue, dancing so joyfully, and with such abandon as though she were drunk enough with color to collapse onto the ground and fall into some eternal pink dream of her own Nirvana.

The old widow formed her lips into a smile, the biggest smile she had ever seen. The image puzzled her, but also caused her own smile to persist, as she, having reached Ganga's magical, forgiving, all-embracing shores, knelt to recite her prayers and light a lamp in the memory of Noor.

Acknowledgements

I first saw the widows of Varanasi in 2009, when they were prohibited from playing Holi, and then later in 2012, when I saw the white widows drenched in the colors of Holi. The image haunted me; I could not forget the sight of their joyous abandon. It was not about the color, it was about the transformation of society. It touched me so deeply that I wrote a book about them. But even that was not enough to capture the beauty of Ma Ganga and the beautiful but scarred city of Varanasi, so I went back and made a movie.

I want to thank all the people who were with me on this journey. My American editor, Paul Assimacopoulos, for spending hundreds of hours with me, helping me translate the emotions that I generally expressed in my native language, and my Indian editor, Nandita Aggarwal, for helping me preserve my tonality and the authenticity of my voice. To Rajbilochan Prasad for seamlessly designing the book.

My heartfelt thanks to India's legendary actress, Neena Gupta for playing the character of Noor so perfectly.

Jitendra Mishra for encouraging me to make the movie – *The Last Color*. I am not sure without him, I would have come this far.

I have to mention the three films that completely inspired me for taking up such a challenge of making one:

ACKNOWLEDGEMENTS

Satyajit Ray's *Pather Panchali*, Mira Nair's *Salaam Bombay* and Drishyam Film's *Masaan*.

Finally, my heartfelt gratitude to the House of Omkar for believing in the story and producing the film.